A LOVE SO DARK

THE DARK REGENCY SERIES BOOK FOUR

CHASITY BOWLIN

To Jonathan.
Thank you for your patience while I slowly
lost my mind on this book.

MAILING LIST

If you'd like to be notified when I have a new release or a sale on backlist titles, please sign up for my mailing list at the link below:

http://eepurl.com/b9B7lL

ALSO BY CHASITY BOWLIN

The Vanishing of Lord Vale

The Missing Marquess of Althorn

The Resurrection of Lady Ramsleigh

The Mystery of Miss Mason

The Awakening of Lord Ambrose

CHAPTER ONE

A GLANCE through the grime covered window revealed the rugged landscape beyond. It was both harsh and beautiful. It was also terrifyingly unfamiliar. She'd never traveled beyond London before, living all of her five and twenty years in a modest neighborhood that only just managed to cling to a bit of respectability. But London was lost to her now, she thought bitterly. Returning to her former home would never again be an option. So they journeyed on to an uncertain future.

Travel, in her opinion, was highly overrated. The constant rocking of the coach had resulted in a persistent and overwhelming nausea. While the last inn they'd stopped at had seemed clean enough and the food appetizing, she'd been afraid to partake of any of it. Now, hunger and illness warred inside her and she wondered if perhaps she hadn't erred in her judgement.

"Is ought amiss, my lady?"

Olympia didn't immediately respond. It wasn't that she was lost in thought, it was simply that she had not become accustomed to being referred to as 'my lady' yet.

"My lady, are you well?" her newly elevated maid asked again.

The other woman's concern penetrated even if the title didn't. Olympia glanced up at her, realizing that her maid had clearly been speaking for sometime. "I'm quite well, Jane—Collins," she corrected. With Olympia's change in station, the young woman who'd been a scullery maid in her aunt and uncle's home had suddenly become her lady's maid, prompting the change of address from her first name to her surname, as was the custom. They both had some adjustments to make, Olympia reminded herself.

Stating that she was fine had been an exaggeration at best and an outright lie at worst. But there was no point in complaining to the maid as little could be done about it in their current situation. "I've simply not become accustomed to my married name yet. My apologies for worrying you."

Collins glanced out the window herself then and shuddered. "Barren place, this."

"It's winter, Collins. I'm sure that in the spring and summer, it will be lovely," Olympia assured her.

Collins' expression was clearly dubious but she replied dutifully. "Yes, Lady Darke."

Olympia, Lady Griffin. Viscountess Darke. It was

certainly going to take some getting used to. She'd been Miss Olympia Daventry for her entire life and had given up the thought of being married, content to remain Daventry until she shuffled off this mortal coil. Or she would have been, had her life at home not become so abysmal that escape of any sort was her only option.

Letting the curtain drop back into place, Olympia settled herself back comfortably on the squab seat, or as comfortably as was possible. The carriage bumped along the rutted road, jarring every aching bone in her body. She placed a hand over her rebellious stomach and willed herself not to vomit.

The journey to her new home was proving more arduous than she'd anticipated, but she reminded herself that it could always be worse. She could still be in her childhood home, now in the possession of her aunt and uncle, suffering their false piety and bitterness. Instead, she was now married to a man she had never met.

Abruptly, the carriage pitched to the left, righted itself, and then pitched again in the opposite direction, this time listing heavily to one side. It slowed immediately and then stopped altogether.

"We've broken a wheel, my lady!" the driver called down.

Olympia sighed. "How far are we from Darkwood Hall?"

"It's two hour still by road, ma'am, but if you cut across the moors, you can be there by dark."

Olympia looked at the leaden and overcast sky. Rain threatened but the prospect of getting wet was not as unappealing as the prospect of being stranded in the infernal carriage for several more hours.

"We will walk, Collins, and leave the coachman here to care for the horses," Olympia stated matter-of-factly.

Collins looked out at the barren and drab landscape and then began to rub her thigh through the fabric of her gown. "I can't, my lady. My leg still pains me something fierce."

Guilt clawed at Olympia. She knew only too well the circumstance in which Collins had been injured. The girl, for there was no denying that she was little more than that regardless of her station, had come to her aid and paid a price for it. By unspoken agreement, neither of them had spoken of that night. Olympia wished to keep it that way. "Very well, Collins. I will go alone. A short walk will allow me to stretch my legs and recover from the rigors of being trapped in this box for such an interminable journey. You may stay behind with a clear conscience."

"If you insist, my lady."

"I do, Collins. Quite firmly," Olympia replied. She would never be so cruel as to insist that the young woman accompany her when clearly, she was unable to do so.

Knocking on the roof of the coach, she called out, "I'm going to go for help, if you could just lower the steps."

"No steps, m'lady!" he called back. "Part of the wheel flew up into 'em when it broke. They're beyond repair."

It was simply getting better and better, Olympia thought rather grimly. The listing side of the carriage was deep in the mud and muck, which meant she'd have to exit through the higher side. Every movement sent the carriage to rocking precariously. Climbing upwards toward the door, she managed to unlatch it and throw it open. It banged against the side of the carriage with the force she'd been required to put behind it. The sound was so loud it nearly deafened her. On the opposite seat, Collins jumped at the sound.

With an alarming lack of skill or grace, Olympia managed to lever herself out of the vehicle and jumped down to the road below. It was only a few feet, but in her present state of exhaustion, even that was a massive effort.

"I'd go for help myself, m'lady, but I'm afraid one of the horses might be lame. I can't leave it," the coachman explained apologetically.

Olympia looked at the horses, all of whom were already grazing happily on grass at the road side. She could question it, but to what end? The man had been useless and half drunk throughout their journey. "Of course. I do not mind the walk. It will be quite refreshing... if you could just point the way?"

He gestured toward a low rock wall that banded the road. "Just over the moors there. You'll see the house soon enough. Right atop a rise and the biggest house in these parts. I'll wait with the horses and the maid until another cart can be sent down."

"Of course," she agreed and then with less grace than enthusiasm, clamored over the rock wall and into the field beyond.

It didn't take her long to realize that the coachman had significantly downplayed the difficulty of the walk. It was a hike, to be precise, over rough and uneven ground heavy with rocks and deep holes that were an invitation to a nasty sprain or worse. Even in her traveling gown and sturdy half boots, she struggled.

The slope was far steeper than it had looked and she was winded by the time she reached the top of the hill. Her feet had slipped multiple times in the wet grass and the mud, leaving her clothes dirty and her hair falling from the simple chignon that Collins had labored over just that morning. Slapping the label of lady's maid on a kitchen girl did not make her one, Olympia reminded herself. And it was precisely because of her that Collins would not have been able to safely remain in her aunt and uncle's home. Elevating the girl's station to lady's maid had been the only way to see them both safely from that house.

Having crested the rise, Olympia took in the vista, more because she needed to catch her breath than because she wished to enjoy the view. The illness prompted by the rocking coach and her decision to simply eschew food altogether had left her feeling weak and less than steady on her feet. The climb had taken what little energy she possessed and the rigors of the journey had wiped out any reserved she had. Of course, she'd been subsisting on a meager diet before that. Her aunt and uncle were miserly with the food budget, buying only the cheapest cuts of meat from the butcher and vegetables that most would simply have discarded.

The thought of food, *real food*, prepared with flavor and taste that would leave her satisfied and happily stuffed had her stomach growling in anticipation. She loved food, Olympia thought. Truly loved it. Cakes, pies, biscuits, scones, thick cuts of pork and roast well seasoned and roasted in a heady sauce, or quail browned to golden perfection. Olympia swayed, weak with hunger. Darkwood Hall, she reminded herself. If she could just get to Darkwood Hall, she would be able to eat real food while sitting on a solid, unmoving surface. That thought spurred her on, prompting her to move forward.

The coachman, if her interpretation was correct, had told the truth. At the top another large hill, on an impressive promontory, stood a large and imposing structure of carved stone, weathered with age to a deep dark gray. Damp as it was, the walls appeared black. A shiver swept through her as she took in the imposing fortress-like appearance of her new home.

After her brief rest to catch her breath and shoring up her wavering courage, she continued on. The fine mist that hung in the air gradually grew heavier and finally gave way to a cold, driving rain. Shivering, teeth chattering, her whole body aching from the arduous journey in the poorly sprung coach, Olympia trudged on.

She stumbled again, several times, falling to her knees in

the damp grass. With her hands planted on the grass, she pushed herself up to a standing position, but her ankle twisted painfully beneath her and sank again to the damp earth. Was this to be the end of her then? Having come so very far, with the house in sight, she would die of cold and exposure right there in the field?

A low rumble reached her ears. At first she thought it was thunder, but it grew louder and closer, and the earth seemed to tremble beneath her feet. Glancing to her right, she saw a horse bearing down on her. The large, black beast was massive beyond description and the darkly cloaked rider on its back only added to the sense of menace.

Whether it was the rain or just recklessness, the rider didn't slow. The horse's massive hooves were dangerously close. Olympia screamed and dove to the right, landing on the muddy ground with enough force to leave her dazed. Her ribs connected painfully with a sharp stone, robbing her of breath.

The horse reared, rising on its hind legs and thrashing in the air. Hooves flashed in front of her. Terrified, Olympia drew herself up into as small a ball as possible as the rider cursed and tried to calm the raging beast.

As abruptly as the terrifying encounter occurred it ended. The sound of crashing hooves stopped.

Cautiously, Olympia rolled onto her back and looked up, blinking against the rain. She wasn't seriously injured, but badly shaken.

"You bloody fool! Do you have any idea what might have happened to you?"

Olympia craned her neck in the direction of the angry shout. She didn't have the breath to reply.

He approached then, having discarded his hat. His hair was just as black as the cloak he wore. His face might have been handsome had his expression not been so fierce.

"Are you hurt?" he demanded. The question itself might have been concerned, but his tone was anything but. Angry. Biting. Harsh.

"I'm fine," she managed to utter breathlessly.

"What the devil are you doing out here?" he asked, offering a hand to help her up.

Olympia accepted it gratefully. Even through their rain soaked gloves, she could feel the heat of his strong hand. As she got to her feet, her ankle crumpled beneath her, refusing to bear weight. Had it not been for his strong arms closing about her, holding her up, she would have fallen again.

"Our carriage broke a wheel," she explained. It was difficult to speak, unnerved as she was by his proximity, by the feeling of his firm chest against her and his arms about her. Haltingly, she finished, "It was closer to cut through the moors than to take the road."

"And your mistress allowed this?" he demanded angrily as he helped her toward a large stone that would provide support for her to lean against. His expression was grim, his lips pressed into a firm and disapproving line. "What sort of person are you employed by?"

Handsome as he was, unnerving as his presence was to her, she would not tolerate anyone speaking to her that way. Was that not the very reason she had left her aunt and uncle's home? "I have no employer. Only employees. The coachman could not leave the horses and my maid complained of a pain in her limb," she snapped, her tone imperious. "I do not understand why you are angry with me! I've done nothing wrong. I was simply walking when you and that beast nearly ran me down!"

"Nothing wrong? Is trespassing no longer illegal, then?" he shot back sarcastically as he stalked back toward the beast in question who was still prancing agitatedly.

With her chin up defiantly she replied as stiffly and with all the imperiousness she could muster, "It isn't trespassing! These are my husband's lands!"

He stopped abruptly, turning back to her. One of his dark brows arced upward as he asked in obvious disbelief, "And who is your husband, madam?"

Drawing herself up to her full height and squaring her shoulders, she replied firmly, "Lord Albus Griffin, Viscount Darke... And who are you, sir?"

He crossed his arms over his chest as if in a challenge and with one peaked eyebrow raised, replied, "I am Lord Albus Leopold Griffin, Viscount Darke!"

Of course he was. Her disastrously poor luck would allow

for nothing else. Olympia started to speak, to say something that would be an appropriate response to learning that the dark, fierce man before her was her husband, but as she opened her mouth, the earth seemed to shift beneath her feet. She grappled for the stone behind her, something to hold on to, but it was no use. Her vision dimmed, blackening around the edges and shrinking down to pinpricks. She could just make out him speaking to her but what he was saying was impossible to comprehend. Her last coherent thought, before unconsciousness claimed her, was that she had never fainted before in her life.

CHAPTER TWO

THE HORSE THUNDERED up the long drive, slowing only when they neared the door and the shocked servants waiting there. It wasn't every day, after all, that their master came riding up with an unconscious woman in his arms.

Two footmen stepped forward and Griffin reluctantly allowed them to take his bride's limp form from his arms. *His bride. His wife.* And he didn't even know her name. He'd asked it, but she'd only stared at him blankly for a second before sinking to the cold ground.

He'd been angry at her recklessness, initially, and at the fact that had he been a less skilled rider, Balthazar could have killed her. Then she'd stumbled due to her turned ankle and he'd caught her. It had been an age since he'd held a woman, felt the undeniable softness of a feminine body pressed against his own. But propriety had demanded that he not prolong that contact, and he'd behaved as any gentleman should. Then she'd uttered the name of her husband. *His* name. And all he'd been able to think was that he could have held her longer, could have savored that feeling more deeply because propriety had no meaning between them.

His first thought, once he'd realized that he hadn't inadvertently killed an innocent young woman, was that she was delectable. Not beautiful, precisely but wholly appealing with her wide dark eyes and a wealth of coffee colored hair that tumbled around her face. Even in her heavy pelisse, her lush curves had been evident and he had immediately longed to see more of her. *All of her.*

It had angered him; that unexpected attraction, that distracting and damning need that he could never give in to. In his anger, he'd lashed out with harsh and biting words, spoken to her in a tone that he had never used even with the laziest of his servants. And she'd fallen, her eyes had glazed over blankly and she'd simply slipped into unconsciousness. Guilt plagued him as he thought of the fact that he, with his rough treatment or his reckless riding over the moors on a stallion that was barely tame, might be responsible for it.

Whatever had occurred, it was more than simply a swoon. She was so cold her skin was practically blue and he couldn't be certain that she hadn't received some injury when Balthazar, his stallion, had been thrashing about. He had enough guilt to contend with already. Bringing an innocent young woman to Darkwood Hall, with its tragic history and hidden secrets, to live out her life in a lonely farce of a marriage were both sin enough already. To do her injury on top of that was simply too much.

Dismounting, Griffin immediately took her into his arms again. He felt strangely possessive and protective, whether it was out of a sense of responsibility for whatever injury she might have sustained or whether it was some instinctive thing prompted by the knowledge that she was *his,* he could not say. Regardless, he was reluctant to entrust her care to anyone else. Given the nature of his household, he had little enough confidence in the ability and the willingness of his servants to offer genuine aid.

"Have hot water and some tea sent to Lady Darke's chambers," he instructed the butler who simply stood there with his mouth agape.

The man sputtered ineffectively for several seconds. "Lady Darke?"

Griffin paused, one booted foot on the bottom stair. "Yes. Lady Darke. I did inform you that I had sent Mr. Swindon to London to procure a bride in my stead and had instructed you to ready the connecting suite. You did follow my instructions, Simms, did you not?"

The butler looked on the verge of an apoplectic fit. "No, my lord. Mrs. Webster and the Viscountess, felt it would be an inefficient use of the servants' time to ready a room when we had no notion of when it was to be occupied."

The fury that filled him at that was spurred by his worry

for the woman in his arms. "Then have the items sent to my chambers... and I will address this issue with both you and Mrs. Webster, and, in her turn, Lady Florence, once my new viscountess is situated. This is *my house*, Simms. I will not be disobeyed again!"

With that, Griffin climbed the stairs. As he neared the top, she stirred, her eyes fluttering open. She was obviously confused, uncertain of her surroundings.

"I have brought you to Darkwood Hall. You'll be safe here," he said softly.

"Safe from what?" she asked.

"Anything that would do you harm," he lied. There were as many dangers within the walls of Darkwood as out, but for the moment, at least, he wanted to offer her a sense of security.

Griffin reached his chambers and a footman opened the door. Stepping inside, he placed her on the bed, ignoring any thoughts of how right it felt to do so. Theirs was not to be a real marriage. That had never been his intent. In fact, his instructions to Swindon had been to find him a bride who would never tempt him to consummate the marriage. It was a path that would lead only to ruin and he already had far too many sins to count against him.

"What is your name?" he asked her softly.

Her eyes opened again. Wide and so very dark that he could lose himself in them, they were framed by a fringe of thick black lashes. They were also achingly innocent, free of any shadows and so very unlike his own.

"Olympia Daventry."

"Griffin," he corrected. "Olympia Griffin."

She blinked up at him then. "Yes. I haven't quite grown accustomed to it yet."

He shouldn't let her. Annulment was the only sensible option. Living with a woman like her, day in and day out, faced with the temptation she afforded, would be hellish. Assuming, of course, that he had the will necessary to resist her. He did not.

"You will," he said simply. "I'll send a maid to assist you into dry clothing of some fashion until your luggage can be reclaimed, along with your erstwhile servants."

"You'll send someone to help them?" she asked.

His lips firmed and he looked down at her pale, wan face. There was no color in her cheeks and there were dark hollows beneath her eyes. But it was the shadows he saw within those dark orbs that entranced him. What suffering had his young bride endured that she'd have such a well of sadness inside her? He was treading in dangerous waters, with swift moving currents that threatened to pull him under. Women, and their ability to get into a man's head, were a path to madness. That was a road he could ill afford to travel.

"They are undeserving of your concern, but yes. I will send someone to fetch them," he reassured her.

"Thank you."

A maid entered then, bearing a tray with tea. Footmen would follow shortly with heated water. "Rest, Olympia. Someone will be in to assist you shortly."

Griffin left the room with a warning glare at the maid who cowed and bobbed her head. His servants were not truly his. They were loyal to his aunt by marriage, Lady Florence Griffin, the now-former Viscountess Darke. The daughter of a bankrupt earl, she was quite content to remain at Darkwood rather than return to the less than sheltering bosom of her family. She would not welcome Olympia. In truth she would not welcome any woman into the house, much less one who was younger and now outranked her.

And then he reflected, there was Mrs. Webster. There was naught to be done for it. The housekeeper could not be discharged for fear that she'd ruin them all. She was privy to secrets that could destroy the Griffin family, financially and socially. It was not beneath her to use that information either. As for Lady Florence, he would exile her to the dower house, if it weren't in a shambles. But he'd pay dearly for it, and in the end, so would his bride.

In the hall, he found one of the women who had sparked his ire. With her steel gray hair swept back into a tight chignon and the black bombazine dress that she wore, she looked rather crow-like. "Mrs. Webster, why were my orders to have her ladyship's chambers readied ignored?"

She lifted her chin, clearly unmoved by his displeasure.

"'Twas wasteful, my lord, until we knew when her ladyship would be arriving."

"And yet she has arrived to a very poor greeting indeed," he chastened. "See to her chambers and see to it that lads from the stables take a cart to fetch her servants and bags. Their carriage is disabled on the road."

"Yes, my lord," the woman said, inclining her head, but there was no mistaking the sneer in her tone or the malice in her eyes.

Griffin started to walk away, but some part of him was so goaded by her obvious disrespect that he simply couldn't refrain from engagement. "I understand that we are at an impasse, Mrs. Webster. You wield an authority in this house that I cannot violate due to fear of repercussion... but do not make my life, or the life of my bride, so uncomfortable that those repercussions become worth the risk. Is that understood?"

She glared at him coldly. "Perfectly, my lord. I will see to it that her ladyship enjoys all the hospitality that Darkwood Hall has to offer."

It was a veiled threat and they both knew it, but he had few options at the moment. "What a sad welcome that will be," he murmured and walked away.

As he rounded the corner, he saw the smirking face of his aunt. Every bloodless confrontation he endured with Mrs. Webster fueled her glee at his misery.

"You've never understood how to deal with her," Florence

said coolly. "Too brash, too bold, and too much of a bore... so very like your late uncle. I wonder if the similarities end there."

Griffin ignored her goading. "The dower house is in poor condition, but don't think I won't send you there... and as far as my bride is concerned, steer clear of her, Florence. Or you'll find out just how bold and brash I can be."

The woman was still laughing as he walked away.

OLYMPIA WATCHED the maid scurry about the all too masculine chamber. The girl appeared fearful, nervous, and utterly cowed. Was her husband such a harsh master, then?

"What is your name, girl?" she asked.

"Marjorie, m'lady," the maid replied, her voice barely above a whisper.

"Marjorie, you've no need to be so fearful. I'm sure his lordship is quite pleased with your performance as a maid."

The young woman gaped at her owlishly for a moment and then bobbed her head. "Yes, m'lady. Quite so. Would you wish me to pour the tea?"

Olympia normally would have poured for herself, but given how shaken she was and how horribly exhausted, it seemed imprudent. The lack of food, the illness prompted by the endless swaying and jerking of the carriage, followed by the cold and the shock of nearly being run down by that giant beast of a horse had taken a heavy toll on her. And lack of sleep, she admitted ruefully. There'd not been a night since leaving her aunt and uncle's home that she hadn't woken in a cold sweat, terrified that it was all some cruel dream she would wake from. All of that, coupled with the shock of coming face to face with her husband, was it any wonder she'd fainted dead away?

Thinking of her husband, Olympia flushed. He was a handsome man, though with his dark countenance and chiseled features, he was also an intimidating one. His manner was less than genteel as well. Abrupt, almost rude, certainly impatient—what sort of husband would he be? What sort of marriage could they possibly have starting off on such ill tidings?

"The tea, m'lady?" the maid repeated. "You want I should pour for you?"

Olympia looked down and realized that the cup in her hand was trembling so badly that the girl couldn't possibly fill it without scalding them both. Placing the cup back on the tray, she forced herself back to the present and away from worries she could do nothing about. "Yes, Marjorie. Thank you."

The girl filled the cup, adding a bit of honey to it, but her hands appeared no steadier than Olympia's own. When the girl returned the teapot to the tray, Olympia lifted her cup and took a long swallow of the heated liquid. It soothed her throat and the warmth spread through her like a blessing. The plate of scones with cream and jam called to her like a siren. Not trusting herself to eat them with even a modicum of manners, she wanted to wait until the young maid left before she inhaled them.

"Lord Darke is not an unkind master, m'lady, no matter what anyone else says of him," the girl whispered, glancing nervously over her shoulder. "But this house is a bleak place. You'd have been better off to never come here, ma'am."

Olympia wanted to press her for further explanation but the door opened and two footmen entered bearing pails of heated water. With them was a woman so fierce and cold in her appearance that it took all of Olympia's will not to simply draw back from her. With her dark gray hair scraped into a tight bun and the uninterrupted severity of her black gown, it was enough to make a body shiver. But it was the air of menace and anger that surrounded her that truly left Olympia shaken.

"Your bath, my lady," the woman said. "I am Mrs. Webster, the housekeeper here. I should advise you that Darkwood Hall is quite old and portions of the house are in ill repair. I would not go about alone if I were you."

It sounded curiously as if she intended for Olympia to be restricted to her chambers. She would not, Olympia vowed silently, ever be in that position again. "And will a servant be available to escort me whenever necessary?"

The woman's already thin lips pressed into a hard line.

"The servants have work enough. Your husband or I, myself will guide you through the house."

"I see," Olympia replied. Her husband could not have departed her company any quicker had the hounds of hell been at his heels. And the idea of willingly spending a minute longer than necessary in the company of the unpleasant, wretched woman before her was off-putting to say the least and torturous at worse.

"You may go, Marjorie," the woman said stiffly. "And in the future, you'll hold your tongue. Lady Darke needs no assurances from you about the nature of her husband... time will reveal all."

Marjorie, fearful and quite chastened from her scolding, left quickly after bobbing a trembling curtsy.

Olympia watched as the housekeeper retreated from the room with one last glower in her direction. Left alone with the water steaming in the tub and no maid to assist her out of her gown, Olympia rose and struggled through the process herself. Luckily, her traveling gown was intended to be removed without assistance. Still, as she limped toward the tub on her swollen and already bruising ankle, she wondered at what she'd gotten herself into. It appeared that she had gone from one untenable situation to another.

"Dear, heavens," she said, sinking into the tub. "What have I done?"

CHAPTER THREE

Olympia awoke with a start, her hand flying to her heart and a scream hovering behind her clenched teeth. It hadn't been the familiar nightmare of her last nights in London that had woken her, but something else.

Sitting up in bed, she surveyed her surroundings with dismay as the reality of where she was sank in. Darkwood Hall. In *her husband's* chamber. With her heart pounding and her blood racing in her veins, she struggled to calm her labored breathing. It was as if she'd run up and down the craggy hills and across the moors that surrounded her here at Darkwood.

Fear was an ugly emotion. And yet it was one she'd become painfully accustomed to over the last few months. But her uncle was not lurking outside her bedchamber door, she reminded herself. She had not dodged his drunken advances after dinner to narrowly escape ruin at his hands. So what had woken her?

Getting out of the bed, she winced as she put weight on her ankle. Testing it, she breathed a sigh of relief when it actually held her weight. Had she imagined the noise? Had it simply been a dream, after all?

No sooner had the thought occurred to her than she heard it again, that same terrifying sound that had pulled her from sleep. The low, animalistic wail echoed over the heavy stone walls and sent shivers down her spine. Was someone injured or ill?

Reaching for her wrapper, she donned it and moved toward the door. In the dark, disoriented as she was, she couldn't be certain which door led to the hall. She tried the first one and drew up short. It was not the corridor, after all, but her husband's dressing room. It was also occupied.

Olympia stared in dawning horror at the man before her. Her face flamed with embarrassment. He wore only breeches and his shirt, open at the neck, revealed a swath of dark skin and crisp black hair. Averting her gaze, she stammered out an apology. "Forgive me. I was unsure which door led to the corridor."

"Why would you be going into the corridor?" he asked. Clearly he was not as perturbed by his state of undress as she was.

"I heard something," she confessed breathlessly. She felt warm, her face flushed and her blood thick in her veins. It wasn't entirely embarrassment that she felt at having caught him in such a state, but it would be foolhardy to lay a name to it. The man was too handsome by far, but his temperament left her uncertain. "It sounded like a scream or a cry for help."

He moved closer to her. So close, in fact, that she could feel the heat emanating from his body and she could smell the scent of him. Leather and sandalwood and something that was just him. It made her nervous, but it also made her curious. Neither was a welcome emotion.

"It is only the wind," he said softly.

She frowned at that too pat answer and glanced up at him, meeting his gaze directly. "I've never heard the wind make such a chilling sound," she stated emphatically. "It sounds like a woman... screaming."

He shook his head, and offered a smile that did not reach his eyes. "In the upper floors of the house, it whistles between cracks in the stone, old archers' slits... It plays tricks on the mind if one permits it to do so."

Lies. They were uttered with practiced ease, but a lack of conviction. Olympia scanned his face, taking in every nuance of his expression. He appeared the soul of sincerity. Uncertain of precisely how she knew that he wasn't speaking the truth, she didn't doubt her instinct on the matter. If she believed him to be lying, he undoubtedly was. Without hesitation, she was utterly certain of it. Challenging him further would not help her cause. Clearly, based on his tone earlier and the fact that he couldn't have left her in his servants' care quickly enough, he was less than pleased with his solicitor's choice of a bride. Questioning his honor so directly would have her sent packing, back to London and the all too certain fate that awaited her in her aunt and uncle's home. "Then I'll learn to ignore it I suppose."

"If you remain here," he answered softly.

Her heartbeat quickened then for a very different reason. Had he already decided to send her away then? The terror that swarmed inside her at that pronouncement left her weak. She'd committed herself fully to making a life at Darkwood Hall. While it was primarily because she had no other option, a part of her had exalted at the idea of having her own home again, of making a life without a falsely pious, drunken and lecherous man stalking her every moment of the day and night.

Forcing herself to speak, to face that terrifying outcome, Olympia asked pointedly, "Where would I go, my lord? I realize we have not spoken about the arrangement handled by your solicitor, but I am your wife. Where else would I reside?" Recalling the ordeal of completing the proxy marriage, crossing the channel to France where the service could be performed legally, then traveling all the way to York-shire to meet a husband who was clearly perturbed at his solicitor's choice—it was all too much, she thought. She'd done all of those things just to have some sense of security and it was simply not to be.

"I meant nothing by it," he offered soothingly. "Only that

perhaps we may go to London or into Liverpool at times and be far from Darkwood Hall."

More lies, she thought. It hadn't been what he meant at all. He wasn't just displeased with his solicitor's choice. He meant to cast her off. On top of the very practical reasons why that terrified her, such as being homeless, impoverished and her reputation never recovering from it, it also stung her already beleaguered pride.

"I do not think that it is what you meant at all. I feel that you meant we would live separately. Or that perhaps you mean to end our arrangement. Am I mistaken, my lord?" It was a bold tactic to address the issue so directly but she had to know.

His heavy sigh was answer enough, as was his downcast gaze. She surmised that he didn't want to look at her directly when he told her he found her wanting.

"I will have to admit that I am considering the possibility, Olympia," he finally uttered in a tone that was far softer than anything she'd yet heard from him. But when he looked up, meeting her gaze so intently, there was a sadness in his voice. "Darkwood Hall is no place for you."

It wasn't that Darkwood Hall wasn't for her. It was that she wasn't for him, she thought bitterly. She'd had a few suitors when she'd been younger, before her parents had passed and her aunt and uncle had relegated her to the role of servant. One she'd been quite hopeful of in fact, but in the end, he'd passed her over for another. A younger woman, prettier, with a slim and petite figure so different from her own overly curved one. Even with the meager rations provided by her relatives, her figure had remained undeniably plump.

It had to be said, to be acknowledged. They were both perfectly aware of what he really meant, she thought. "Your solicitor, Mr. Swindon, led me to believe that you were not concerned with either the beauty or fortune of the woman you chose to marry... but rather that expedience was the most important quality. Was he mistaken, then? We have yet to discuss my lack of fortune, which leaves only my appearance as your point of contention... I am sorry you find me displeasing."

IT TOOK Griffin a moment to process what she'd said. The truth of the matter was that any higher functioning of his mind had ceased the moment she'd appeared in the doorway, dressed in a borrowed nightrail and a wrapper that had seen better days. He was acutely aware of the lush curves hidden beneath those thin layers of cloth. His palms itched with the need to trace each hill and valley, to learn the contours of her waist and the flare of her hips, to test the weight of her breasts in his hands. The need was so sharp it rendered him near senseless.

She'd been on his mind for the better part of the evening

as he labored over his decisions. What was he to do with her? Could he set her up in a house in London or Liverpool and allow her to live an independent life? Swindon had been instructed to find a spinster, a woman with no prospects for whom the sham he offered would be a blessing. Olympia was young, lovely, and should have a husband to dote on her and children to spoil. Those were things he could never give her.

And yet, he couldn't forget the sensation of her in his arms, or the porcelain perfection of her skin as he'd stared down at her. If he touched her, would it be as soft as it appeared? *If* he touched her? From the moment she'd entered his dressing room, his thoughts had been preoccupied with how few layers of clothing stood between them and with the thought that it was the first night he would be under the same roof with his new bride. And she had been in his bed. Alone.

As her words penetrated the fog of lust that had robbed him of the ability to speak coherently, he shook his head. "You mistake me, Olympia. There is nothing about you that is displeasing... Did Swindon not mention to you that my bride's lack of fortune or beauty was of no import because this was to be a marriage in name only?"

Her eyebrows arched and her eyes widened in surprise. "That was *not* mentioned, my lord. Whyever would you seek such an arrangement?"

"My reasons are not entirely my own and thus I am not at liberty to share them," he replied. Even if he were, he wouldn't tell her. The very idea of seeing either pity for him or fear of him in her eyes was more than he could bear. "I had instructed Swindon that he should seek out a plain woman, a spinster... one who would have no other prospects and for whom this would be a boon."

"And so he did," she replied.

"No. He most assuredly did not. Olympia, you are many things, but plain could never be one of them... and that will only make our arrangement more difficult," he continued. How did one tell an innocent woman that their marriage could not possibly work precisely because he desired her too much? He'd wanted her from the moment he'd first laid eyes upon her—facing him down in the rain, refusing to be cowed by him in spite of all she'd been through. He'd thought her utterly magnificent, if mad. And then she'd fainted. Recalling the weight of her in his arms, the sensation of her breath fanning over his cheek as he'd carried her to his horse, his body responded in a way that should have shamed him. His desire for her had been instant and intense. Every encounter with her, every moment in her presence, only amplified it.

"You have been too long without the company of women if you do not find me plain," she replied. "Plain, plump, and poor. Those have been my defining features for the better part of my life. And at five and twenty without a suitor in sight, I can assure you, I most definitely qualify as a spinster."

He had no argument for that. "I could tell you that you are beautiful but you would not believe me. So I will tell you that I find you quite pretty, instead... Appealing to me in a way that no woman has for a very long time. It is a paltry compliment, but true enough I suppose. You have a quiet prettiness that draws a man, but I cannot afford to be drawn to you. *You* cannot afford it."

"What a strange thing to say!" She stared up at him quizzically. Whether she moved closer or he did, he could not say, but they were standing so near that he could see the gooseflesh rise on her skin as another round of wails filtered down the darkened halls. She turned in the direction of the sound and swayed on her feet. He reached out to steady her, but as his hands closed over her forearms, feeling the delicate bones beneath soft, silken skin, he instantly regretted it.

The spark between them flared to glorious life, or perhaps he simply wished to believe that to be true. It justified his actions when he dipped his head and pressed his lips against hers. The taste of her lips was impossibly sweet. Soft and pliant beneath him, she didn't resist, but perhaps out of shock or ignorance, she did not immediately respond either. He wanted her to. The need to awaken that fire in her, though it was a horrible mistake, compelled him. He wanted her to burn for him just as he burned for her.

Griffin tugged her closer, pressing their bodies together as he explored the tender curve of her mouth. A shudder rippled through her and she sank against him, her lush curves molding against him. It was the worst kind of folly, but for that moment, he was beyond caring.

His hands moved from her forearms, down to her waist,

settled on the curve of her hips. Boldly, he swept his tongue beyond the seam of her lips, tasting her fully. She gasped and the spell was broken. Her abrupt retreat had her stumbling, but as he reached for her, she held up one hand to still him.

"I'm quite all right," she said. "I've no need of your assistance."

"Olympia, it was only a kiss," he said. The lie burned on his tongue. There was no 'only' between the two of them. That simple kiss had incited his passion beyond any trick employed by the most skilled of courtesans. Olympia, innocent, untried and all the sweeter for it, was driving him to the brink of madness. "I didn't mean to frighten you."

She glared at him. "Do I appear frightened? Am I cowed? No, my lord, I am not, but neither am I a fool. You've said yourself that this was never to be a real marriage... more to the point, you've said you aren't certain if you mean to continue this marriage at all."

"I did," he admitted grudgingly. Her anger was entirely justified. She'd upended her entire life so that he might claim an inheritance contingent upon his marriage. Now, because he could not control his own ravenous libido, he threatened to upend it yet again.

"Then I suggest, my lord," she continued, each word bitten out in quiet indignation, "that before you bestow any more kisses, you decide once and for all whether or not you mean to cast me off. I can be rejected or I can be ruined, but I refuse to be both."

There was nothing he could say in response to that. He'd acted rashly and abominably. He should see it as a blessing that she possessed more sense than he did at the moment. "I wish this were simpler… or that I were at liberty to share these ugly truths with you."

"Then do so. Or do not. But do not feel entitled to a husband's rights if you refuse to be a husband at all."

"I do not feel entitled," he corrected. "It was an impulse. As much as I should regret it, I do not. That single moment has been brighter than any other in my life for sometime. I am sorry you are upset, but find myself incapable of being sorry for my actions."

She blinked at him, her wide dark eyes clouding with confusion. Finally, she admitted, "I have no idea what to make of this. Or you. I simply do not understand at all. You say I am not plain, and yet you say it almost as if it is an accusation, that because you do not find me so, I have wronged you in some way! And then you kiss me as if—as if…" She trailed off, clearly unable to provide further insight.

"As if I intend to consummate our union?" he provided.

"Yes!" she snapped. "What am I supposed to do, my lord? How should I respond in this situation where I am both desired and reviled?"

"You are not reviled. Not in the least. But I am not free to be the kind of husband you deserve. Fate has certainly played a cruel joke on me… Go back to bed, Olympia. If you hear any more noises in the night, know that they are harmless to you, but this house is not. It is unsafe to wander around in the dark."

She stared at him for a moment, clearly confused by his behavior before retreating once more to the safety of his chamber. He listened to the door close, but she did not lock it. She should have, he thought. If she had any notion of the nature of his thoughts, or of just how deeply that single kiss had stirred him, she would have run from him. She would have bolted and barricaded the door.

The temptation of her was too much. The servants would have her chamber readied on the morrow. A few walls between them would not be nearly enough for his peace of mind.

In another life, he thought bitterly, she was just the type of woman who would have drawn him. Strong minded and strong in her convictions, but with a sense of calm about her that soothed him, that offered the promise of a peaceful and happy life. But it wasn't simply her demeanor that appealed to him. Nor was it just her intelligence, which she appeared to have in abundance. Olympia possessed a quiet beauty and a figure that invoked every carnal instinct within him.

A wife, children, a happy and peaceful home. Those were the things a man expected to have in life, the things that he strived for. But the promise of those things had long been gone from his life. There was no hope of keeping his distance, but it was imperative that he continually remind himself why theirs could never be the marriage he'd envisioned as a young man, when hope still had a place in his life.

The sound of low, keening wails interrupted his lustful thoughts and prompted another curse. The latest potions were not working. She was growing more restless by the day, but the nights were infinitely worse. There would be more long days spent in the conservatory, studying the many treatises on herbs and plants and mixing one concoction after another. He would have to talk to Mrs. Webster and see what could be done in the meantime.

Griffin glanced once more at the door to his chamber and cursed. He grabbed the candelabra from the table and left via the servants' entrance. Traversing the narrow stairs, he headed for the conservatory and his studies. Work would be the only reprieve he'd have from his thoughts and foolish dreams.

CHAPTER FOUR

It had been two days since Olympia had arrived at Darkwood Hall and those two days had been rife with misery.
Restricted to her bed the first day because of her ankle and
because she wished to avoid further conflict with either the
housekeeper or Lord Darke, she was now no longer able or
willing to hide in her room. There was a pall hanging over the
house, a tension that seemed to fill every nook and cranny of
what should have been a grand estate but instead seemed a
dark and dreary place.

The nights were the worst, Olympia reflected. The
strange cries and moans that seemed to fill the upper floors of
the house were haunting. Such pain and misery was impossible to ignore, and yet ignore it she did because it had been
made quite clear to that to do otherwise would have severe
repercussions. Her position was too tenuous by far to court

the ire of either her new husband or his dragon of a housekeeper.

The better part of the night had been spent lying awake in her bed with a pillow pressed to her ears as she tried to block out those awful sounds. Of course, that wasn't the only reason sleep had eluded her. She was keenly aware of her husband lying in his bed in the room next to hers. After the charged exchange in his dressing room on her first night there, she'd been unable to think of anything else. Lies, kisses, and confrontation — all followed by complete avoidance. Would nothing ever be simple between them, she wondered?

Collins brushed her hair, clucking her tongue over the snarls in it. "I wish I could have braided it last night, m'lady. It wouldn't have these nasty snarls in it now. You've a head of hair to be the envy of any woman, and a poor maid to help you care for it."

"You're doing a fine job, Collins... but if you wish to return to being a kitchen maid—."

"No, m'lady!" the young woman protested. "A position like this one is something I never dreamed of. I'll do better! I promise, I will!"

"I'm not dismissing you, Collins. Only offering that if it causes you too much distress, you may take another position in the house that you feel suits you better... I prefer simpler hairstyles," Olympia stated firmly.

Collins said nothing else, but her lips trembled slightly as she gave a sharp nod and returned to her task. When at last her hair was combed out and tied back in a simple ribbon, Olympia rose from her dressing table and looked around for her shawl. Darkwood Hall was drafty and damp, but it wasn't that which left her cold and shivering.

He'd lied to her about what she'd heard. Those sounds she'd heard had not been the wind. They'd been, not human exactly, but close enough. No animal could have made such sounds, but if it had indeed been a woman that Olympia heard in the night, she was broken. Fractured beyond anything Olympia could ken. That sound haunted her. It wasn't something she was sure she'd ever forget, but it was something that she never wanted to hear again. Had he lied to protect himself, to hide his own misdeeds? It was an option she could not overlook. It also made the ease with which she'd all but forgotten herself in his arms even more alarming.

"You don't seem quite right this morning, my lady. Was his lordship not kind to you?"

"His lordship has been cordial, Collins. But we've barely spoken to one another given my illness yesterday," Olympia evaded. It wasn't entirely a lie, she reasoned. "I can't seem to place where I've left my shawl. Did you put it away?"

"No, your ladyship... But I saw you get it out earlier," Collins replied with a puzzled tone.

"Check the wardrobe, just in case. Perhaps I put it away and forgot."

The maid bobbed her head and turned to check the wardrobe, emerging with Olympia's shawl. If Collins said she hadn't put it away, Olympia believed her. The girl had no reason to lie and her trust in the maid was implicit. It had to be. Which meant someone had been in her room.

"Collins, be certain that my chamber is locked when we're not here... It feels very strange to me."

"Yes, ladyship... It is most strange. I can't help but feel—." The girl broke off abruptly and turned her head away.

"What, Collins? What isn't you can't help but feel?"

"It's a bit like when your uncle was skulking about. That's the way it feels, anyway. Like he's watching or lurking. Hiding in the shadows and waiting to pounce. Do you not feel it?"

SHE DID. Every waking moment since coming to Darkwood Hall, she felt it. In taking the girl on as a maid, she'd had to ask for Mr. Swindon's approval, but it had been necessary. She couldn't leave the girl behind to face the awful consequences of what they'd done. He'd granted permission on the condition that he interviewed the girl to be certain she was a suitable employee for the Viscount.

"Collins, did Mr. Swindon say anything to you about his lordship when he agreed to hire you?" she asked.

"No, m'lady. He said nothing to me beyond asking about where I'd been employed past and if my current employers were satisfied with me... I had to lie to him a bit, m'lady. Is it a bad thing, I've done?"

Olympia's stomach pitched at the reminder. "No, Collins. And prior to that evening, your work had been most satisfactory to my aunt and uncle... as satisfying as anything else was to them, at any rate. They are both horribly dissatisfied people in general."

Collins clutched the shawl in her hands, her eyes wide and tears threatening. "You aunt, to be sure still is... but your uncle, I doubt he's much dissatisfied with anything these days."

Olympia said nothing further. A part of her wanted to offer reassurances, to say that everything would be fine. But she neither knew nor believed it and thus couldn't force herself to utter the words.

Collins sighed and began straightening Olympia's meager wardrobe. Eventually it would have to be seen to, but for the time being she had enough clothing of suitable quality that she would not embarrass her husband should they have callers.

As Collins straightened the shawl over Olympia's shoulder, she added, "I was told nothing about his lordship, but was told to be cautious in this house... was warned of strange goings on."

Olympia shivered at that, naturally relating to the idea of strange goings on to the wailing she'd heard the previous night. "Did he say what sort of strange goings on?"

"No, m'lady. Just warned me to be careful and not to be wandering about inside the house or out... My grandmother was from these parts. She told tale of beasties here. Giant hounds what could rip a man apart. I'll not be traipsing about the countryside alone."

Olympia's eyebrows shot up in surprise. "Really, and you didn't think to warn me of that before I left the carriage alone yesterday to go wandering around the countryside? Did you not think that would be a pertinent warning then?"

Collins looked at the floor. "I never believed her, m'lady. Just tall tales is all. And I reckoned you'd be brave enough to face down anything."

There was no point in being angry at the girl and no point in rehashing things that were already said and done. "I am going down to breakfast."

Once in the corridor, Olympia did not head down the hallway toward the main staircase, but instead went in the opposite direction. At the end of the hall, it split abruptly, with narrower hallways going off to the right and to the left. As she was deciding which way to go, a door at the end of the left corridor opened and Mrs. Webster appeared. The woman stopped abruptly.

"What are you doing here?" she demanded, her voice brusque and clearly perturbed.

The woman's tone was sharp and the fact that she did not use Olympia's title indicated just how little regard she had for her as the new lady of the house. Telling the terrifying house-keeper that she was searching for the source of the cries she'd heard in the night was clearly not an option. So, Olympia lied. "I'm quite lost, I fear. I must have turned the wrong way when I left my chamber."

"Then might I suggest you turn around and go the other direction," the housekeeper snapped.

"What is through that door?" Olympia persisted.

"That wing of the house is closed, madam."

"Really? Why were you coming and going from it then?" she demanded. She would have a straight answer from the woman.

The housekeeper's jaw tensed and her already pinched face became positively hollowed by it. "Inventory, my lady. The rooms are closed off because they are never used, but there are still many valuable objects. It is my duty to ensure that no one in this house abuses his lordship's trust!"

It was a pat answer, one that had the woman not been so thoroughly contemptuous of his lordship and herself that Olympia might have been able to believe. Clearly, Mrs. Webster had little use for either of them.

"And is this something you do routinely?" she asked.

The woman bristled further. "Would you like an accounting of how I spend the hours of my day, then?"

"No, Mrs. Webster. But if I am to be mistress of this household, the running of it should be familiar to me. Don't you agree?" Olympia felt a mild victory there, for she'd left the woman with no other option but to agree with her. To do otherwise would clearly see her fired.

The thrill of victory was short-lived. Mrs. Webster smiled

coolly, a mocking expression. "You will never run this house, my lady. As every Viscountess Darke before you, your position here will be purely ornamental. *I* run this house. Just as my mother did and my grandmother before her. If you feel so inclined, ask his lordship. He will tell you precisely how secure my position is here and precisely how little you will be involved with the day to day routine of Darkwood Hall."

She'd never had a servant speak to her so boldly in her life. Olympia was livid. "You overstep, Mrs. Webster!"

The woman moved closer, and while she was thin, she towered over Olympia. As she leaned in, her voice dropped to no more than a whisper, but there was no mistaking the malice in it. "No, madam. *You* have overstepped. A new bride... but not yet a wife. I know where his lordship slept last night. I also know he never intends to make you his wife in the true sense of the word. Your place here is precarious at best. I would not make sweeping demands were I you."

Olympia said nothing. In truth there was no response for that. The housekeeper had said nothing that was untrue, though how she'd gleaned such information was a mystery. It was clear that the woman was ruthless enough to use it to her advantage, however. Without the protection of her station and with her tenuous position in the house, Olympia was left with little recourse. A sinking feeling settled into her stomach. Things were far more wrong at Darkwood than she had realized.

~

GRIFFIN RUBBED HIS EYES. He was beyond tired. Spending half the night in the conservatory and another portion of it in the small room he'd converted into a laboratory, exhaustion was quickly claiming him. But exhaustion would be the only possible inducement for sleep. Even then, he was well aware that he would likely be plagued with dreams of her.

His wife was not the most beautiful woman he'd ever seen, and yet, he'd never felt such an instantaneous desire for any woman. Without even attempting to do so, she'd inflamed him to the point of idiocy.

It didn't help that he'd been isolated from society for a very long time because of his situation. It had been years since he'd been in the company of a woman that was neither relative nor employee. To now find himself in such close proximity to a woman that he found immensely attractive but that also, in the legal sense, had every right to desire, was a particular kind of torment.

Picking up the small vial that contained what he could only hope would be a solution, Griffin tucked it into his hand before making his way to the breakfast room. He would give the new potion to Mrs. Webster. It was too late to use it for the morning, but he'd ask her to substitute it in the afternoon. Perhaps it would allow for a quieter evening, one that wouldn't send his new bride in search of answers.

There were decisions to be made. Did he continue the

farce of a marriage or did he instruct Swindon to being the process of annulment? He'd given up any hope of maintaining a platonic relationship, a marriage in name only. He'd known from the very moment he set eyes on Olympia that would be impossible, but he had not foreseen how quickly his will would succumb to temptation. If she was to remain untouched, she would have to leave Darkwood Hall immediately and forever.

Entering the small dining room that was traditionally reserved for breakfast, but that he'd taken to using for all of his meals, he stopped short inside the door. Olympia was already there. The cascade of dark hair falling over her shoulders, hanging almost to her waist, fueled a dozen fantasies as he envisioned it spread out over the pillow, tangled about them as he took her, or wrapped in his fist as her mouth moved on him. They were fantasies, he reminded himself, and nothing more. What he wanted from her and what he could have were entirely different things.

She turned, as if sensing his perusal, and offered a cordial smile and a murmured 'good morning' as she took her seat. With her hair down and in a simple braid she looked young enough to make his thoughts even more shameful, yet that did nothing to stop them. The feeling of her body pressed against him, of the sweetness of her lips beneath his own, were still ever present in his mind. Even now, taking in the porcelain perfection of her skin, the soft curves of her face and the temptation of her full lips, he was hard pressed not to give in to his more base desires. The longing, the desire he felt for her, was instantaneous. It roared to life with the ferocity and speed of an inferno.

At his lack of response to her greeting, she simply smiled brighter and carried the burden of conversation by asking softly, "Did you sleep well?"

"As well as I deserve," he replied evasively as he moved to the sideboard to fill a plate. He needed space between them, distance. And he needed to not be facing her when the evidence of her effect on him was clearly visible.

"I am glad to have a moment to speak with you," she said.

"Oh? Do I need to be scolded for something else? Taken to task for my lack of morals or accused of some other perfidy?" he asked. While his tone was conversational, the words held bite.

She ignored that. "We are in an unusual situation, my lord. You needed a bride, and I needed to establish a home for myself where I would not be dependent on the charity of my relatives. Regardless of anything else that has occurred between us or our perceptions of one another, those circumstances have not changed."

Griffin had already surmised that he would not be able to annul the marriage. Legally, it was within his right as it had not been consummated. But his response to the mere suggestion was visceral. She belonged to him already, whether either of them wished to admit it. Still, he allowed her to make her case. "That is true enough," he agreed.

"My lord, my suggestion is that we reside here together for one month. If at that time, you still wish to send me away, then do so as your wife. We can live separately if you desire and my needs are quite modest."

"I should remain married to you, set you up in your own home, and leave you to your own devices," he surmised.

She flushed but her jaw hardened with determination as she continued. "Only if it is your wish, my lord. I will be quite content to remain here at Darkwood Hall."

That prompted his eyebrows to raise in disbelief. "No one is ever content at Darkwood Hall. I daresay the rocks would march from the fields to flee it were they able."

She sighed heavily. "Then I shall not say I will be content. I shall simply offer the truth with all that is left of my pride... I have nowhere else to go."

The admission had cost her dearly. He could see it in the slight deflation of her previously squared shoulders and in the way she avoided his gaze. Pity was not something she would ever accept, and in truth, was not something he would offer. But he was not without feeling and it saddened him for her that her lot in life had become such that her only option had been marriage sight unseen to a man she did not know the first thing about.

He'd goaded her thoughtlessly, and in doing so, he'd hurt her in ways she would not be quick to forgive. "Whatever occurs, you will always have a home and always be provided for," he offered. "That is all I can promise at this time."

"It is enough," she said softly. "Thank you."

Griffin nodded. His appetite was gone entirely. Food held no appeal for him and the one thing he hungered for was completely off limits. "I am going for a ride. I will see you at dinner," he said and quickly moved to escape the damning pleasure he took in her presence. She was dangerous to him in ways he had not envisioned and he would need to proceed cautiously.

CHAPTER FIVE

OLYMPIA HAD BEEN STARING down at the table, but when she looked up, she pinned him with a sharp and direct gaze. It was clear that she had something on her mind, and he undoubtedly would be put on the spot.

"I understand that you have not had time to make a decision on whether or not I am to remain here with you, my lord, but do you have some notion of how long a time will be required for you to decide?"

He had. From the moment he'd walked into that room, there was simply no turning back. It was a foolhardy decision, one that they would both come to regret he was certain, but having her and keeping her were inevitable. Since their soul scorching kiss, she'd become as necessary to him as breathing. Her presence had invaded his home, invaded his mind. His awareness of her had continued to grow. Where she was, what she was doing, how she was being treated in his strange and not entirely welcoming home—all of those things had consumed his thoughts. And in seeing to her comfort, in doing the things that a husband would do, it cemented that relationship even further in his mind.

To deny it was futile. "For better or worse, Olympia, you will remain here. But there are rules to follow if this is to work... and once you hear them, it may be your wish to leave."

She put down her fork and folded her hands neatly in her lap. "Very well."

Griffin turned to the door and the footmen standing there. "Leave us." They looked at one another before doing his bidding. Undoubtedly they were off to report to Mrs. Webster. The woman was out of control. Something would have to be done. Moving toward the table, he took a seat across from Olympia, one that would allow them to converse more easily than if he'd sat at the head of the table as usual.

"Your rules, my lord?"

He smiled slightly. "The first one is to stop 'my lording' me every time we speak. You will call me Griffin. I prefer it. I have not held the title for very long and find I am not accustomed to it yet."

She frowned at that. "Were you not anticipating becoming Viscount Darke, then?"

"No," he replied. "The title was initially my uncle's, and it should have gone to my cousin or his younger brother, but he... there was a tragedy," he finished lamely. "Suffice to say, I had not expected the title and find myself acclimating slowly." His tone made it quite clear that he intended to say no more on the subject and he only hoped she would not press him. The lurid tale was not fit for her ears.

"I see. And your second rule?"

This one would be more difficult. "There are areas of the house that are unsafe. I will give you a tour later and show you where you may and may not go within these walls... Also, the moors are dangerous, incredibly so. The grass grows so tall that it conceals deep crevices in the earth and prevents you from being able to tell whether the earth beneath is firm or simply a well concealed bog. You should not go out alone."

The tension emanating from her was palpable. Her shoulders squared and her chin came up while her eyes hardened as if ready for battle. She was extraordinary, he thought.

"Am I to be a prisoner here, then?" she demanded.

"Not at all. If you wish to go out, you may, I would only ask that you alert someone to where you are going and take a servant with you who is familiar with the area," he replied in an attempt to reassure her. "But I should warn you, we are not well received in the village."

"Why?"

"The tragedy," he replied coolly. "Small minds give rise to great rumors. If you must go there, pay them no heed... that is a suggestion, not a rule."

"I feel I should be making notes," she responded.

"There is only one other rule, but I suppose it falls more under the heading of a demand," he answered.

"Do go on. I find myself on tenterhooks," she replied with complete sarcasm.

"I admit to my own foolishness in even considering the possibility that I could have a marriage in name only with a woman I find so wholly appealing. But regardless of whether or not our marriage is consummated, Olympia, precautions will be taken... We will have no children."

CHAPTER SIX

SHE'D BEEN TOLD NOT to wander, but as the source of her instruction had been Mrs. Webster, Olympia felt fully justified in ignoring the edict. A housekeeper had no jurisdiction over her, she reasoned.

The brief exchange with Lord Darke over breakfast had offered her some peace of mind. Of course, trusting him to keep his word might be an awful mistake, but it was all she had to cling to at the moment. Even a false sense of security was better than living in terror of being turned out into the streets.

Not even Collins knew what she was about. In truth, it wasn't a proud moment for her. But she needed a strategic advantage and that meant doing a little spying on her own. Slipping along the same corridor where she'd had her earlier confrontation with Mrs. Webster, Olympia ducked into an alcove to keep watch and observe her new household.

After what seemed like hours, the door at the end of the hall opened. Olympia held her breath as the housekeeper moved past her, the black bombazine of her gown swishing with her brisk steps. Peeking around the corner, Olympia quickly shrank back when the woman paused and glanced over her shoulder.

Fearing she'd been caught, Olympia braced for battle, but instead Mrs. Webster simply walked over to a marquetry table in the hall. She ran her fingers over the top of it, grimaced at the dust there and then went on her way.

Letting out a sigh of relief, Olympia immediately dashed out toward the door the woman had recently exited. It was unlocked, which surprised her, but also worried her. Would Mrs. Webster come back to check? It was a risk she would have to take.

Ducking through the door, she closed it firmly behind her. She leaned against it for a brief moment to catch her breath and still her racing heart. Clearly a life of crime was not in her future as just sneaking into a forbidden area of the house had her on the verge of apoplexy.

The corridor stretched before her. Dust covered the floor and cobwebs draped from the ceiling. But in the center of the hallway, there was a wide swath of floor free of any dust at all. It was marked with the occasional footprint that strayed from the path. Staring at those footprints, Olympia recognized that one would clearly have to be Mrs. Webster's. The other, much larger and clearly belonging to a man, could only be her husband's.

Making her way as stealthily as possible, Olympia tried the first door on the left. It opened easily enough. Peering inside, she saw nothing but furniture draped in Holland cloths. Closing the door, she moved along the corridor, investigating each one. It wasn't until she neared the end that she found what she was looking for. The room was stacked high with trunks and books. Personal items were interspersed amongst everything else. It was the haphazard lot of a household hastily moved into storage.

Stepping carefully over the threshold to avoid leaving visible prints in front of the door in the hallway, Olympia stepped into the room and closed the door. The quiet immediately set her on edge. There was no sound of bustling servants. None of the general liveliness of a house well occupied. That room was as silent as a tomb.

"And if Mrs. Webster comes back and locks the door, it could well be *your* tomb," she told herself. To that end, Olympia began her search. She went through each stack of books, looking for anything of a personal nature. When they failed to yield anything, she moved onto the trunks. She'd just searched the third one when the wailing began.

It was much louder, and so much clearer this close to the source. Olympia longed to go to her, whoever she was, and offer some comfort, but it would surely not end well for her.

Without a doubt, those cries would bring Mrs. Webster rushing back, which meant her time was limited. Dusting off her skirts, she rose, but her recently injured ankle betrayed her. She stumbled, catching herself on the edge of the trunk and the lining ripped beneath her hand. A small packet of letters fell out.

Olympia picked them up carefully and then examined the torn lining. Hidden behind it was also a slim book, clearly a journal. Satisfied with her haul for the moment, she tidied up behind her. Just as she reached for the door, and opened it just a crack, she heard footsteps in the hall.

Terrified to move or even breathe, she stood there with her face pressed to that tiny opening. The housekeeper rushed past, halting at another closed door at the end of the corridor. As Olympia watched, she removed the ring of keys at her waist and unlocked the door. A flight of stairs was visible as she opened the door and disappeared inside.

Olympia didn't hesitate for a second. She opened the door, stepped out carefully into the cleared swatch of floor in the center and ran. In her soft kid slippers, her feet were nearly silent on the floor as she hurried toward the door. Once in the main hallway again, she ducked back into the same alcove where she'd hidden earlier and tried to catch her breath.

Running in stays, especially when terrified of being caught, was torture. Her ankle pained her something fierce and she was bound to come face to face with Mrs. Webster at any moment.

The door at the end of the hall opened again, and Olympia leaned back against the wall. She would surely be caught and then any agreement she might have reached with Lord Darke would surely be null and void. He'd send her packing. The fate of any woman turned out by her husband was bound to be a gruesome one.

But once again, Mrs. Webster simply brushed past her, never pausing as she deposited a vial in the pocket of her dress, just beneath the clinking chatelaine at her waist. As Mrs. Webster's steps receded, the wailing and shrieking began to lessen. What, Olympia wondered, was in that bottle?

After waiting several moments to be sure the housekeeper was well and truly gone, Olympia drew her shawl from her shoulder and bundled her purloined items in the center and folded them up inside. Reaching beneath the hem of her gown, she secured the shawl about her waist, and then smoothed her dress. If she were caught, she would simply say she was out for a walk. It was a much more palatable explanation than snooping through forbidden rooms in a house where she was barely welcome to start.

Stepping from her hiding place, she made her way along the corridor. Before turning the corner into the main hall that would take her back to her own chamber, Olympia peered carefully around. Mrs. Webster stood near the door to her chamber. She'd raised her hand to knock, just as Collins popped out of one of the many servants' doors that lined the hallway.

"Where is your mistress?" Mrs. Webster demanded.

"She's sleeping," Collins lied smoothly.

"I knocked... quite loudly," Mrs. Webster stated. "Her door is locked!"

"She had no wish to be disturbed," Collins replied. Her gaze skated past Mrs. Webster to Olympia's pale face just visible as she peeked around the corner.

"Then why are you here?" The housekeeper was clearly having none of it.

"Because it is the time that she asked me to wake her," Collins retorted.

"Then I shall wait," Mrs. Webster stated smugly.

Collins squared her thin shoulders and met the housekeeper's hard gaze. "M'lady's instructions, specifically, Mrs. Webster, were that she had no wish to be disturbed by you. I will inform her that you wish to speak to her, but whether she wishes to speak to you is her choice, I reckon!"

"You cheeky girl! I'll have you sacked for this!"

Collins never blinked. "You can't. The only person who can send me packing is her ladyship. And as I'm only doing what she asked, I doubt she'll see it your way."

Mrs. Webster appeared to be on the verge of an apoplectic fit. Olympia could see her trembling from her present vantage point. The woman's hand flew back as if she meant to strike the maid, but before it could happen a masculine voice called out.

"What the devil is going on?" Lord Darke shouted as he opened his chamber door. "Mrs. Webster?"

"This girl is refusing to wake her mistress!"

"As her mistress undoubtedly instructed her, Mrs. Webster. You may have the run of the house but you do not have the run of a peer or his wife," Lord Darke reminded her imperiously.

As Olympia looked on, the housekeeper glanced back over her shoulder toward her hiding place. If she'd turned just a few more inches, Olympia would have been spotted. Finally, the woman glared at Lord Darke one last time then swept past all of them toward the main staircase, as if she had every right to use it.

Never in all of Olympia's dealings with the upper class had a servant, even one in such a lofty position as housekeeper, made so free with the house that employed her. Eventually, Lord Darke retreated into his room. Warily, Olympia left her hiding place and approached Collins who still stood in the hallway looking like a ghost.

"I thought she'd take my head clean off," the younger woman muttered.

"I think she'd prefer to have mine," Olympia replied in a conspiratorial tone. "Why is my chamber door locked?"

Collins blushed. "It isn't the first time I caught her

sniffing around this door today. She was waiting to go through your things when you went down to breakfast."

Olympia wanted to be angry, but since she'd just done the very same thing, she simply moved on. "But she has a key!"

Collins smiled. "It isn't just locked with a key, my lady. I put a chair under the knob. I'll be going through the servants' entrance through your dressing room and will let you in that way."

Collins was proving far more resourceful than she'd ever imagined. Hairstyling could be taught, but what she'd just done could not. "How did you know she didn't use the servant's entrance?"

The maid shrugged, a slight lift of her thin and frail looking shoulders. "She won't sneak in that way, because she feels it's her right to go in like quality... bold as brass, my lady. Or so I suspect."

"Let me in quickly. We're going to have a very long afternoon," Olympia said.

She felt exposed in the hallway, as if there were eyes watching and ears listening in to every word that was said.

CHAPTER SEVEN

A SHORT TIME LATER GRIFFIN, now clad in his riding clothes, exited his chambers and headed for the stairs. Mrs. Webster's boldness was proving far more problematic than he'd imagined. He would not allow her to run roughshod over Olympia, but he was in a delicate position. The things she knew about his family could result in catastrophic ruin both socially and financially. He was over a barrel in more ways than one. And at the moment, rather than face up to the problems that were clearly going nowhere, he elected to run away. A fast gallop over the fields on Balthazar would do much to improve his mood.

The side benefit of his ride would be getting out of the house and away from the temptation that Olympia presented. He needed five minutes' peace, five minutes of not thinking of her in the chamber next to his, wondering what she was doing, what she was wearing—or more importantly, what she was not wearing.

As he stepped outside, the cold air hit him squarely. A storm was brewing. Snow would be falling before the night was through and judging by the leaden sky, there would be more than enough of it to keep them housebound for some time. There would be no sending her away, he realized. Without time to make proper arrangements, it wouldn't be safe and whatever else occurred, he meant to be certain that she was protected, at the very least.

Once his horse was saddled, he mounted quickly and took off over the moors. The path he used was one he knew well, the same one where he'd encountered Olympia only two days earlier. In only forty-eight hours, she'd turned his whole world upside down. But her presence and the resulting upheaval in his world was *exciting* and so very little in his world had excited him in a very long time.

The first flakes fell as he whipped the stallion around and headed toward the road. The rumbling of carriage wheels reached him long before the carriage rounded the bend. It would be Florence, of course, he thought bitterly.

A feeling of dread settled inside him, making him want to ride on, to simply gallop away from all of it and forget all of his problems. But that wasn't possible, because it would mean leaving Olympia alone in a house with Mrs. Webster and the viper who was even now rounding the bend to Darkwood Hall. His aunt by marriage, the young and troublesome widow of his late uncle had returned from far too short a visit to their neighbor and her only friend, Lady Darlington. She would bring misery and histrionics with her, as they were her constant companion.

Griffin uttered a word he would never have said in polite company and tugged at the reins and turned Balthazar back toward the house. He had a responsibility to see to her safety and comfort and he would not shirk it, even at the loss of his own.

The ride home was frigid, the weather turning quickly and the ground covered in a thin dusting of snow by the time he reached the stables. Griffin prayed they would not get a heavy snow. The last thing he wanted was to be part of a captive audience for her dramatics.

In her room, Olympia carefully removed the first from the packet of letters and unfolded it. They were not addressed to anyone and there was no signature at the end. As she read, she quickly began to understand why. The passionate prose was clearly a communication between secret lovers. It wasn't just intimate, it was also quite risqué. Her face heated as she read the detailed account of love and desire.

"What did you find, my lady?" Collins asked.

A particularly heated phrase had Olympia stammering

her response. "Love letters... though there's no indication of who they might have been written to or by."

"Maybe the letters was to or from the person who wrote in that book," Collins suggested helpfully as she worked her needle through the torn fabric of Olympia's traveling dress. The many falls she'd taken during her hike over the moors and nearly being trampled by Viscount Darke's horse had taken quite a toll on the garment.

It was a rather good suggestion. Setting aside the letters and uncertain exactly why she was so reluctant to do so, Olympia reached for the book. Inscribed on the inside book plate was a name. Miss Patrice Landon. The handwriting in the journal appeared quite different from that of the letters, indicating that perhaps she'd been the recipient of such ardent devotion and desire.

Who was Patrice Landon and why were such personal and private letters hidden in the confines of a series of forbidden rooms within the bowels of Darkwood Hall?

A commotion in the hallway prompted Olympia to hide the letters and journal. She tucked them into the sewing basket that she despised and quickly grabbed up a piece of embroidery that she'd been working on for far too long already. It was a hopeless case.

Collins eyed the hopelessly mangled piece of cloth with something akin to horror. "Who did that?"

"I did," Olympia snapped. "I know it's horrible! Now hush!"

Olympia had no sooner uttered the admonishment when a knock sounded at the door. It swung inward and Mrs. Webster marched in as if it was well within her right to do so. "Lady Florence Griffin, Viscountess Darke has returned to the hall. It would be appropriate for you to greet her and welcome her upon her return!"

"Viscountess Darke?"

Mrs. Webster smiled coolly. "I misspoke, my lady. Lady Florence Griffin has returned."

With that bold pronouncement, Mrs. Webster turned on her heel and left. It was a command, clearly, and one that Olympia had no clear way to get out of it because the house-keeper was right. It was her place to greet Lady Florence.

Shoving the embroidery aside, Olympia rose and straight-ened her gown. "I have the distinct impression this is not going to go well. Mrs. Webster seems quite pleased to have my husband's aunt in residence... I fear I have yet another enemy under this roof, Collins. Be certain those letters and the journal are well hidden. I can't help but feel they are important and I do not want anyone to abscond with them before I can gather what I need from them."

"Yes, m'lady," Collins said and rose from her own perfect embroidery. "M'lady?"

"Yes, Collins?"

"I had awful dreams last night, m'lady. And I can't help but thinking about what happened before we left. Do you think he's recovered, your uncle?"

Olympia felt the blood drain from her face. "I doubt it. I doubt that he shall ever recover, Collins. And we must not speak of it. There are people in this house who would use anything against us. No more talk of our lives in London. They are over and done. We will make the best of our new lives here. Understood?"

The maid nodded her agreement and ducked her head to hide the stray tears that escaped her. It wasn't love for her previous employer. Olympia knew that. It was the same fear that haunted her—that one day the truth of what had happened to him would come out and they would both have to pay for it.

Stepping into the corridor, Olympia once again found herself face to face with her husband. He had avoided her for the most part, and had certainly avoided being alone with her. A small squeak escaped her as she stumbled toward him, brought up short by her own surprise.

He reached out, his hand closing over her forearm to steady her. The heat of it brought to mind the letters she'd just read, words detailing the longing for a heated touch, the pleasure in a caress, in a kiss.

"Are you so eager for my company, then?" he asked. "Or is it my touch that has you so eager, Olympia?"

Olympia could feel the heat creeping up her neck as a blush stained her cheeks.

"I simply wasn't expecting to see you lurking in the hall," she retorted.

"Speaking of lurking in the hall," he said. "Mrs. Webster is on a tear, ranting to the rafters about you allegedly spying and lurking about. Please do try not to antagonize her."

"My every drawn breath antagonizes her."

He didn't laugh, but his lips quirked upward in a sardonic smile. "That is quite true," he agreed. "But let us try to cohabit peaceably, shall we?"

"Is that possible?" she asked frankly. She seemed to always be irritating him. Her very presence was vexing to him and he'd made it quite apparent that he was eager enough to be free of her. And yet, he looked at her in a way that made her blush and stammer, that made the blood race in her veins.

"We shall soon find out," he said. "The snow has just begun to fall. We will be trapped here together... whether for a day or a week is anyone's guess. In considering the implications of that, I realized one very more important fact."

"And what is that, my lord?"

"That I rather like the idea of being trapped with you for days."

"I don't understand," she said.

"I thought I could resist you... I thought," Griffin continued, "That I could live in this house with you and not consummate our union. But I cannot. I will not. I mean to make you my wife in every sense. But there is one thing you must know... we will never have children. Precautions will be taken to ensure it."

He spoke so matter-of-factly about things she simply

could not. It also sparked a dozen questions in her mind. What sort of precautions? How did one go about preventing a child when the very activity he spoke of was intended to create one? More to the point, would she be content with that? For now, certainly, but at some point, would she want more, would she feel that overwhelming maternal need? What would happen then?

"I see... Before I agree to this, as clearly your man failed to enlighten me sufficiently as to what precisely would be awaiting me here at Darkwood Hall, there are things that I need assurances of," she said.

"I will do my best to offer them," he replied evenly. Yet his hand never stopped moving on her arm, his fingers tracing delicate lines over her skin.

Olympia looked at him directly, challengingly even, as she tried to curb her response to him. She would not be put off and she would not be lied to and she would not be distracted by the tenderness of his touch. "Those sounds I heard last night were most assuredly not the wind. What is going on in this house?"

He stared back, considering his answer carefully, it seemed to her. After what seemed an interminable pause in the conversation, he finally spoke. "I cannot tell you precisely what is happening. There are secrets in this house, but they are not mine to share. What I can tell you is that you have nothing to fear in this house... whatever is happening is not as it would seem, but it is not evil or wicked or anything else that some might say to you. Will that suffice as an explanation for now?"

He'd turned it around her and now she was stuck. She had no real bargaining power. There was nowhere else for her to go. Even assuming that her aunt and uncle, assuming he survived, would take her in again after she'd married a stranger by proxy and run off to the wilds of northern Yorkshire, she had no desire to return to their home and the fate that awaited her there. "For now," she relented. "And Mrs. Webster? Can you assure me that she isn't evil or wicked?"

"No, I cannot."

Surprised, Olympia blinked at him rather owlishly at his bald statement. She hadn't expected that he would simply admit it readily. The woman chilled her to the bone and clearly he had no great affection for her either. "Why do you permit her to remain?"

"For yet more reasons that I am not at liberty to explain," he replied. "She is a permanent fixture in this house and her authority, while not absolute, is significant. I will speak to her if she has been rude to you."

And the entire household would view her as a weak, mealy mouthed thing who required her husband to stand up for her in all things. It simply would not do. "That isn't necessary. I will deal with Mrs. Webster as is needed... But I mean to run this household, my lord," Olympia said emphatically. "I will never again live as a guest in my own home or bow to others in it."

"Is that why you consented to marry a man you've never met? Because you were being treated so in your own home?"

Olympia decided that if he could have secrets then she was entitled to her own as well. "My reasons are my own to share, but I don't mean to. Not now or ever. And that is all I mean to say on the matter."

A slight smile curved his lips and all she could think of was the kiss they'd shared— how it had felt when he'd pressed those lips to hers before. She understood desire, in theory, at least. But she'd never experienced it. Shocked as she had been, it hadn't progressed to that point in his dressing room, but she was certainly aware that it could have. Given his stated intentions, it was something she should be glad of. If they were to consummate their union, then surely having a husband one desired was a stroke of good luck.

"Touché" he replied softly. "I won't press you for answers and you will afford me the same courtesy. You will remain at Darkwood Hall as my wife. And you will have all the protection my title affords."

Hearing it phrased in that way brought home the reality of it to her in a way that she hadn't yet been able to comprehend. She'd gone from an impoverished spinster living on the uncertain charity of unkind relations to being the wife of a titled nobleman. But she'd made her bed, so to speak, and it was time to lie in it. The unfortunate phrasing of her own thoughts, brought another subject to mind. Consummation. He hadn't said when he intended for this to happen, but she could only imagine it would be soon. It left her feeling curious and terrified all at once.

"Are we in agreement then? You will have your secrets and I will have mine... and I will have you."

His voice had dipped lower, the rich baritone sweeping over her skin in a way that raised goosebumps over her flesh. Heat unfurled in her belly at the sensual gleam in his eyes as his gaze roamed over her. If he could elicit such a response with only a look, what would happen when he actually touched her?

Her breath shuddered out as she forced herself to answer, "Yes, my lord... Griffin."

His hand slid down her harm, lacing her fingers through his. With the pad of his thumb he stroked the tender skin at the inside of her wrist. "I enjoy the sound of my name on your lips."

Her blush deepened. "I cannot be sure, but I feel you are being quite scandalous right now."

His laughter was as much a surprise to him as it was to her. "I haven't done that in some time," he remarked.

"Laughed?"

"Laughed or been scandalous. I look forward to doing infinitely more of both," he said as he rose from the table. "Until tonight, Olympia. I will see you at dinner."

Watching him go, Olympia sank back against the door. She'd gone from one fine mess to another and hadn't the faintest idea how to navigate the murky waters she now found herself in. And her only ally was the unlikely Collins.

"I fervently wish," she muttered, "that I knew how to curse."

AFTER LEAVING Olympia in the hall, Griffin sought out the woman who was currently making his life a misery. He dreaded it, but he had to face her down at some point. Mrs. Webster had always been somewhat paranoid. It was nothing new. But her current episode appeared more vitriolic than most.

Mrs. Webster had been a source of torment for the ages. While he hadn't spent the entirety of his childhood at Dark-wood, he'd been there often enough to form a mutual enmity with her. During his visits there as a child, she'd hovered over him, boxing his ears, scolding him incessantly and, in short, inhibiting any joy for all those in her vicinity.

Since the tragedy, since the death of his cousins and his uncle and the awful event that had robbed his sister of any semblance of her humanity, things had grown significantly worse. She was the only one who knew the true circumstances of their deaths and was lording it over him. If she made those awful details common knowledge he would be ruined. He'd invested heavily in several local enterprises in Liverpool and if they got wind of it, it would be detrimental to them all. He could not allow that to happen, allow those businesses to fail and people to lose their livelihoods because of his involvement.

He found her near the entrance to the east wing, bearing a lunch tray. "I have something for you to try, a variation on what we were using before... it should calm her," he said.

"You said that about the last one," she snapped back.

"I am an amateur botanist, Mrs. Webster, not a physician. We are both out of our depths here," he replied evenly, though he wanted to wring the woman's neck.

She nodded. "Very well. I will give her the new potion and we shall see if the night is calmer than the last. If it is not, what then, my lord?"

"Then we try something else," he said.

"Your new bride is curious." Her voice was laden with accusation.

"What would you have me do, Mrs. Webster? I had to marry to claim the inheritance from Aunt Honoria. Without it, with the ramshackle way my late uncle managed finances, and the fury with which Lady Florence can spend money, Darkwood would fall into ruin and decay!"

"I understand your need to marry, and I thank you for making such a sacrifice to keep Darkwood flourishing," she said. It was the closest to praise he'd ever received from her. "But your choice leaves something to be desired. She's a headstrong girl. Nothing but trouble will come of it.... her lurking and spying. She'll bring ruin upon this house, my lord!"

He was living in a nest of vipers. A power hungry house-keeper, a dowager aunt younger than he was himself, who dressed like a trollop and behaved worse, servants in rebel-lion, a curious and willful wife—there was no winning in his present situation. "I have spoken to Lady Darke. She under-stands that Darkwood is not a place to wander. But you will speak to her with the respect her position deserves," he said. "I cannot have her treated so."

"Then I suggest you brew a potion to calm her, as well," the housekeeper snapped again. She turned on her heel then, unlocked the door, and swept into the forbidden wing of Darkwood Hall.

CHAPTER EIGHT

OLYMPIA GATHERED her composure after the encounter with her husband before making her way down the stairs. She had no idea what was awaiting her in the form of the dowager, but she was not eager to find out. In her mind's eye, she envisioned some aging crone with a cane and an imperious stare. It was, after all, what the very word *dowager* implied. But instinct told her this would be something very different.

At the bottom of the stairs, the butler, Simms met her with a grim visage. She was learning that it was his natural expression. "Lady Darke will join you in the drawing room, my lady. She'll be down momentarily."

Olympia had brought her wretched embroidery with her, not because she enjoyed it, but because it would give her something to occupy her time while she waited for the dowa-

ger. She had no notion of what to expect, though she anticipated a battle axe of a woman, a compatriot of Mrs. Webster.

But the woman who swept into the room nearly a quarter
of an hour later was not at all like Mrs. Webster. In fact, she'd
never seen a woman as beautiful as the one before her. She
possessed the kind of self-satisfied and practiced loveliness
that inspired hatred in other women, Olympia was honest
enough to admit she was not immune to that response herself.

The dowager's was gown was of the first stare of fashion,
if somewhat scandalously low cut, particularly for day wear,
and her blonde curls were arranged in such a way that
Olympia could only regret the reminder of Collins' complete
lack of skill at hairdressing. She possessed a slim figure, but
one that was still adequately curved and feminine. The
graceful movements as she all but floated across the room
were enough to make any mere mortal woman despise her.

"Good morning, my dear," she cooed in a voice as soft as
an angel's. "You must be Olympia! Oh, that naughty Griffin!
He should have told me you were coming!"

"I am Olympia," she said. "And Griffin appears to have
been quite naughty because he didn't warn me of your arrival
either."

Her laugher, which naturally had to sound like the
tinkling of a bell, rang out. "How very droll you are! I didn't
tell the dear boy that I was coming... I do so love surprises!"

Olympia reckoned that the *dear boy* was a good five years
older than the woman before her, if he was a day. "How nice

for you then that this house has borne witness to so many of late," Olympia stated softly. There was something about the previous Viscountess—the very young, very lovely and very possibly viperous Viscountess—that set Olympia's teeth on edge. She hadn't gone out much in society, but when she had, she'd seen enough of that sort to understand when a woman was talking out of both sides of her mouth.

"We've not had many surprises of late," Lady Florence offered with a pretty pout that was just a shade too practiced to be genuine. "Not since my dear husband's passing! And even then, they were rarely pleasant. But Griffin has been kind enough to let me remain here!"

She sounded ridiculously jovial about the passing of her husband rather than grief stricken. Commenting on that would only antagonize the woman or create an ugly scene, Olympia opted for diplomacy, though it pained her to do so. "I see. It is very kind of him. And I'm terribly sorry for your loss."

The woman waved a hand dismissively. Her smile might have been lovely, had her eyes not been utterly devoid of any warmth. "Dear Roger. A lovely man when we met... but not at all well. Griffin is very like him, I think. In many ways. Alas, most of the Darke men are not long for this world."

It wasn't precisely a threat, but it was near enough that Olympia was quite uncomfortable. "He appears to be the picture of health."

At that, the other woman laughed snidely. "And so they

all do... until they don't. Many people in this family suffer a *peculiar* type of sickness. It occurs very suddenly, but I am unaware of anyone ever recovering from it."

"Again, I can but offer my condolences to you," Olympia repeated, uncertain of anything else to say. The woman appeared gleeful at the demise of her own husband and step-sons. She was positively aglow at the notion that a similar affliction might befall Olympia's own husband. And yet she remained at Darkwood Hall on his charity, which, based upon the cut of the woman's gown, was remarkably generous.

"I'm still quite young and not unattractive yet," she offered with a smile. "If circumstances demand it, I might consider taking another husband. You certainly set yourself up very well! No title, no fortune... and while you're an attractive enough girl, your looks aren't exactly the fashion right now, are they? And yet you snagged a well-heeled gentleman with a title!"

"I snagged no one," Olympia retorted, unable to tolerate the false joviality a moment longer. Wrapping a barb in a thin veil of silk did not make it less sharp. "An offer was made and Mr. Swindon assured me that I met all the requirements of Lord Darke."

"Yes," Florence said, hissing the word between her teeth. "A plain, long in the tooth, unappealing spinster that he would never be tempted to bed... I can certainly see where Mr. Swindon might have attributed such damning traits to you."

The words cut like jagged shards of glass, burrowing beneath the skin and promising more discomfort to come. Had her husband expressed to his aunt that an unappealing wife was his wish? Or had the woman simply eavesdropped? Or had Mrs. Webster provided that bit of insight? Olympia didn't want to make accusations against anyone and she didn't know Griffin well enough to defend him. But she certainly had a well formed opinion of the woman before her.

Looking down at the embroidery in her lap, Olympia replied, "I believe I will retire for a bit. I've shed enough blood at the end of my own needle... I won't be bearing the brunt of yours any longer."

Florence giggled again. "Don't run off on my account."

Olympia looked squarely at her when she spoke as calmly and confidently as she could. "I've no wish to cross swords with you, nor do I wish to engage in some endless battle where we are constantly clawing at one another through the veil of polite conversation. I've greeted you as is my duty. Now we shall endeavor to avoid one another as best as possible... Good afternoon, Lady Florence."

"What possessed you to accept an offer of marriage from a man you'd never met?"

Olympia paused, her steps faltering. The question had been posed thoughtfully. It wasn't idle curiosity at all, but a woman fishing for the truth. "My aunt and uncle were less than generous," she said, which was certainly the truth. "I was tired of living as a servant in a home where I had once been the exalted daughter." It was technically the truth as well. If she'd left out the fact that she'd done grave injury to her uncle when he attempted to rape her and that her newly promoted lady's maid had come to her aid in covering up the crime by helping Olympia place his broken body at the foot of the stairs, then so be it.

"That would certainly be a difficult transition," Lady Florence said, clucking her tongue in false sympathy. "Still it seems a bit extreme. Such a desolate place you've brought yourself to! It's almost as if you wished to be as far from London as possible."

"I've always preferred the country," Olympia lied. "The air, usually, is much better. But not here... not in this room."

Lady Florence noted the barb and smiled. "This is going to be ever so much fun! You have a secret," she accused gleefully. "I don't know it is yet, but I will. And when I do, you'll come to heel."

Olympia's blood ran cold at the threat, but she brazened it out. "You are as paranoid as Mrs. Webster. If you'll excuse me, Lady Florence, I'm sure there is something, somewhere within these walls that requires my attention."

"You needn't pretty it up on my account," Lady Florence spoke plainly for the first time. "We are enemies, Lady Darke. You threaten my position here. And I will always be a threat to you... tis the simply the way of the world. A beautiful woman can *always* take what a plain woman possesses."

She possessed nothing, Olympia thought grimly, so there was nothing for her to steal. "You are not a beautiful woman... You are rotten inside. Like the pretty, red skin on a spoiled apple. Good day, Lady Florence."

As she exited the drawing room, she could hear Lady Florence's satisfied giggle behind her. With her fists clenched so tightly that her nails were digging into her palms, she made her way toward the stairs only to encounter the wraithlike and terrifying figure of Mrs. Webster at the foot. Never in her life had she been in a house where servants were so readily seen. No one hid below stairs, no one scurried away when their employers entered a room. It was as if the servants had total control of the house and Lord Darke rather than the other way around.

"She's put out that you're here," Mrs. Webster said with cold disdain. "Thought she'd just trade one Lord Darke for another and go on being the Viscountess."

"Well, I'm not pleased about her presence at the moment either, am I? She's his aunt, for goodness sake!" Olympia retorted sharply. She was in no mood for word games or crossing swords with either of the women who clearly felt they had a more secure position at Darkwood than she did herself.

Mrs. Webster's lips thinned in a pale and sickly imitation of a smile. "Only by marriage, and only for a very short time. Perhaps you should ask Lord Darke how it was she came to be in this desolate place to snare his uncle? As for the two of them, it would be scandalous to be certain, and would require special permission from the bishop, but it could be done. In the meantime, she'll continue to act as if she's still the lady of the house and entitled to it."

"And you will let her, undoubtedly," Olympia snapped. "Tell me, Mrs. Webster, do you always gossip about your betters?"

Mrs. Webster stared down at her nose with all the haughty disdain of a queen. "She is not my better. Neither are you. I would be careful of her, Lady Darke. Her pretty face hides a devious mind."

Olympia shook her head in disbelief. "I cannot countenance that you are trying to help me! No, on the contrary, I think you are simply trying to intimidate me further than you already have. I'm not so easily cowed, Mrs. Webster. Good day!"

"More's the pity, Lady Darke. More's the pity."

Olympia watched the woman walk away, a thin and shadowy figure disappearing into the gloomy corridors without a backward glance. She'd thought that leaving her childhood home, freeing herself from the fear and uncertainty wrought by her uncle, and brought to a head before her hurried marriage, would offer her peace. She'd never imagined that she might find herself in a place just as menacing in an entirely different manner.

⁓

GRIFFIN WAS IN HIS CHAMBER, half dressed when the knock sounded. Assuming it to be a servant or, as some traitorous part of his brain suggested, Olympia, he called out for entry. He regretted it instantly. The scent of a familiar perfume reached him long before she did.

Florence.

"You shouldn't be in here," he said. "It isn't proper."

She gave him a coy smile as she moved about the room, touching things, trailing her fingers suggestively over any object that could be considered remotely phallic. It left him entirely unmoved. He knew her to be a viper, soulless and untrustworthy. Nothing else mattered.

"You haven't missed me even a little in my absence?" she asked, her lips forming a soft, pouty moue.

"No. I have not. I would say I hardly notice your absence but the house was unaccountably peaceful while you were gone. Get out, Florence."

She laughed gaily. "Peaceful? Hardly. Not with your poor, mad sister wailing to beat the band!"

"Florence, I warn you," he uttered through clenched teeth, "Do not speak of her so!"

"Whyever not, Griffin? Cassandra is poor, she is mad and she is your sister. I've said nothing that is untrue, and quite honestly, I am not without sympathy for her plight. I, better than anyone, know just how much damage your uncle could inflict upon a woman!"

He closed his eyes in disgust. "Speak your piece, Florence, and get out!"

"Send her away."

"No."

She smiled at him, her face a vision of perfection and her heart blacker than anyone he'd ever known. "You didn't even ask who I meant," she protested. "I was not speaking of your dear sister but your new bride. Send her away!"

"Whether you spoke of Cassandra or Olympia, my answer would remain the same. There is only one woman in this house I mean to send away and that is you. As soon as the weather has cleared, you will go to the dower house or back to Liverpool. I'll leave the choice to you. But you will never again cross the threshold of Darkwood Hall. Is that clear?"

The small vase she'd been holding and fondling so suggestively came flying at his head. "Bastard!"

"Bitch," he replied reasonably.

"Shall I tell her then?" Florence asked. "Shall I tell your meek, little bride that you once proposed to me? That you professed your love so gallantly and so perfectly that I was swept away by the romance of it all?"

"You will say nothing to Olympia about our former engagement. In fact, you will not speak to her at all!"

"Oh, we've spoken already. I might have even let slip that I tried to convince you to wed me to satisfy the terms of

Honoria's will. I bet she'd be very put out to learn that you were once completely enamored of me."

What woman wouldn't? She would be living under the same roof as a woman he'd once been engaged to marry. If he was lucky, she would simply stop speaking to him. If he was unlucky, and historically speaking that seemed the more likely outcome, she'd pitch half the contents of the house straight at his head. "What do you want, Florence? What is it that will buy your silence?"

"Increase my allowance... and hire a footman that I took a fancy to at Lady Jane Darlington's house. He's a veritable beast in bed. And you know how much I like that."

It took all that he had not to choke the life out of her. "When you move to the dower house, I will hire him as your footman there. But not before. And I'll look into raising your allowance, but I will not pauper myself or the estate for you fripperies."

She snarled, her beautiful face twisting into a gruesome and angry mask. It was a more accurate reflection of her true self than anything he'd ever seen. "Be wary of offending me, Griffin. If you court my ire, I possess all the information needed to ruin you... and your plain, little bride."

Griffin cursed under his breath. "Leave her be, Florence, or so help me I will toss you out into the snow myself!"

"I will see you at dinner," she said.

"No. You will not. You will take a tray in your room and I

will make your excuses," he said. "I'm not going to have you tormenting her there!"

~

OLYMPIA HAD TAKEN a minor detour to the library before returning to her room. Upon her entrance, she found Collins coming from her dressing room nestled between her chamber and Lord Darke's. She was white as a sheet and appeared nervous.

"Collins, has something happened?"

"No, m'lady," the maid said, shaking her head vigorously. "Just got a bit spooked is all. This house is so big and so drafty, and all them tall tales from my grandmother started wafting through my head while I was alone up here. It's nothing."

Relieved at the explanation, Olympia nodded. "Fetch me those letters and the journal Collins, and then return an hour before dinner. I mean to find out all I can from them!"

"Yes, m'lady... The other Lady Darke, the one was married to Lord Darke's uncle—." The maid broke off abruptly.

"Yes, Collins? What about her?"

"Don't trust her, m'lady. Not as far as you can throw her."

Olympia nodded. "I have no intention of trusting anyone in this house save for you. And thank you, Collins... for everything."

Looking much relieved, the maid fetched the books from

where she'd hidden them, tucked carefully into the lining under the chair that sat before the window. Olympia accepted them from her and then sat down at her small writing desk to begin her study of them. She had the feeling that whatever information was contained within them would be very important.

CHAPTER NINE

OLYMPIA DRESSED for dinner with care. She was acutely aware of the fact that she would have to withstand the presence of Lady Florence and she wanted—no, she *needed*—to put her best foot forward. It was a kind of armor, really. And it did truly feel as if she were on the verge of battle.

She hadn't seen Griffin since their encounter in the hall, when he'd announced his decision to make theirs a marriage in truth. It was mostly by her own design that she'd remained hidden in her room for the remainder of the day to avoid any further conflicts with either Lady Florence or Mrs. Webster. Neither woman was to be trusted and while her place at Darkwood Hall was becoming more certain, that only increased their enmity. With Collins as her only true ally, she was sadly outmatched and she knew it.

While her chambers were grand and luxurious, after a

certain number of hours, they still felt like a prison. The only bright spot in the entire ordeal was the realization that it had once been Lady Florence's chamber and she'd had to forfeit it. It was something of a consolation prize.

Olympia reflected that the room was certainly finer than any place she'd ever called her own before. The modest town-house that had belonged to her parents had been comfortable and more than adequate for their needs, but it hadn't been overly luxurious.

The room was done in rich shades of apricot and blue. The carpet and the drapes complemented one another perfectly. The bed curtains were of the same fabric that covered the windows and the furniture was all intricately carved and quite lovely. The frescoed ceiling would take some getting used to, she thought. The nymphs and satyrs appeared to be leering down at her. It was as feminine as Lord Darke's chamber had been masculine.

Would he join her in her bed, or would he expect her to come to his?

It wasn't the first unbidden question to come to her mind about what her husband might expect of her. Her traitorous mind had tormented her with such thoughts throughout the afternoon. A part of her was eager to learn, to explore the notion of passion and desire. Another part of her simply wanted it all done. The uncertainty of it all made her nervous. Would he expect her in his bed that night? A trai-torous part of her hoped that he would.

The gown she'd chosen was her best one, purchased just before she left London with money provided by Mr. Swindon. Made for another lady who had failed to collect it from the dressmaker, Collins had altered it for her. Whatever complaints she had about the maid, her skill with the needle was not one of them.

The claret silk molded to her curves, emphasizing the fullness of her bosom and cascading over her hips. It could not have fit her better had it been made specifically for her.

"You've done a marvelous job, Collins. Thank you."

The young woman stopped in the midst of putting away her day dress. Her eyes widened and her lips formed a perfect 'O'. "You're very welcome, m'lady. Always enjoyed sewing. It's a special treat to work on a gown so fine."

"Do you make dresses, then?" Olympia asked, recalling how very fashionably Lady Florence had dressed. She could never hope to compete with the blonde beauty, but it wouldn't hurt to be as well armed as possible.

"I can, m'lady. But we've no fabric to work with here."

Olympia sighed. "Fabric is easy enough to obtain. We'll go to the village... though I hear we will have a less than warm welcome."

Collins nodded emphatically. "You've got that aright, m'lady. The servants do talk here. More than a bit. They all whisper about a tragedy. Something happened with the last Viscount. It's all whispers and glances, but none of 'em will say what. Though they are all stirred up a bit with the other

Lady Darke coming back. But they all stop talking as soon as they see me. I reckon they know where my loyalties are."

Olympia understood the maid's frustration. All the vague comments and references to tragedy with no one ever actually just saying what they meant was enough to drive one mad. And while it might have been idle curiosity to Collins, for Olympia, it was something else. She felt compelled to know, riddled with questions and curiosity that would give her no peace. All of it was centered firmly around the man she had married, and whether or not he could be trusted. The secrets of Darkwood Hall weighed heavily on her. They weighed heavily on her husband, too. She sensed that in him; that he struggled with some inner pain. But sympathy for him could be costly and she vowed to guard her heart carefully.

Catching Collins' eye in the mirror, Olympia posed the question casually, as if the answer meant nothing to her. "And what of the previous Lord Darke's widow... have they said aught of her?"

Collins, though young, was no one's fool. Her lips primmed in disapproval as she placed several items in the armoire. "Oh, they say plenty about her, my lady. A few of the footmen are right friendly with her... seems they were just as friendly before she became a widow. The maids don't seem to like her overmuch... has a temper, I heard one say. Will toss a room till it looks like it's been burgled just because her breakfast tray came with tea instead of chocolate."

The gong rang for dinner before Olympia could press

for more information. Rising from her dressing table, Olympia took one final look in the mirror. Collins skill with a needle was without equaled but her skill with the curling tongs was far from enviable. With that in mind, her hair had been fashioned into a simple coronet and laced with ribbon. It was far from fashionable but it would simply have to do.

As she descended the stairs, Griffin was waiting for her near the bottom. When she reached him, she accepted his proffered arm only too well aware that she was in fact accepting so much more. They were proclaiming, to all there to witness, that they were joined. And while the household consisted only of servants, servants' gossip could travel far and wide.

"That gown is very fetching... but not nearly as fetching as the woman who wears it." The words were uttered with a smile and a challenge. He was daring her to deny his statement.

"You're being quite charming," Olympia observed archly. "I wasn't aware it was in your repertoire."

"I have many things in my repertoire that you are not yet aware of," Griffin replied smoothly, but with a wicked gleam in his eyes that left little doubt as to his meaning.

"You're being scandalous... again. You do realize that if you keep this up it will be all over the county by tomorrow that we're in a love match?" she asked.

"And why shouldn't it be?" he asked softly.

"Because we are not in a love match, or in love, even. We are expedient for one another," she answered.

GRIFFIN'S SMILE faded as he led Olympia into the formal dining room. People would talk, but it was something he'd grown accustomed to. Their family had long been a source of gossip for those with nothing better to occupy their time. Was it fair to bring her into that world? To make her an object of ridicule and speculation? But did he have any choice? His great-aunt had known of his decision never to marry and because of that, she'd constructed her will in such a fashion that he would have no alternative but to do that very thing.

Aunt Honoria had felt all the talk of family curses was nonsense. She'd believed none of it even when confronted with evidence to the contrary. So she'd tied her money up in a neat little package that could only be opened in the event he wed, knowing all the while that he would have no choice but to comply or the family estate would fall into utter ruin and the lives of the farmers that depended on the estate would be ruined as well.

So now he found himself saddled with a bride who incited lust in him like no other woman he'd ever known, but who, for reasons he would never be able to share with her, he should not touch. It would have been amusing had it not been so damnably frustrating.

In the dining room, he paused at the end of the table and allowed her to survey the room. It would be their first dinner together there. She would not like the room. Few did. Cold, stark, it harkened back to Darkwood's history as a fortress in years gone by. The swords and spears covering the walls gave testament to it.

"It's a bit bloodthirsty, isn't it?" she asked as she took in the rather austere decor.

He could tell her the true history of the room—that his uncle murdered his two sons and took his own life there beneath the carved family crest. That he'd shot Cassandra in the head and she'd survived only because the gun had malfunctioned, but that the wound had destroyed her humanity and left her a feral shell of a woman, broken beyond repair. It would win him no favors and would not endear him, or his home, to her.

"It is a room designed to intimidate," he offered instead. "Has it worked?"

"If your housekeeper has failed on that score, nothing else will succeed.... Unless, Lady Florence is dining with us. In that case, I've developed a sudden and debilitating megrim."

A rusty chuckle escaped him. He hadn't laughed in so long that the sound was unfamiliar to his ears. And yet it was becoming a regular occurrence around her. Had his life really become so devoid of any enjoyment? Yes, he thought. It had. For years, he'd focused on his work, or finding the right combination of herbs and plants to offer her peace. Nothing had worked. The more he'd focused on it, the more desperate he'd become for answers that were not forthcoming. Then there was the loss of his parents, and the awful tragedy of his uncle. Joy was an unfamiliar and long absent visitor to him anymore.

The fact that his home was a battlefield pocked by the bloodless skirmishes between the women of the household did not help. Both Lady Florence and Mrs. Webster were impossible to deal with and yet he did deal with them both on a daily basis. It would drive any man mad, and he was close enough to that already. Rather than dwell on that topic, he instead took in Olympia's appearance, allowing his gaze to roam over her freely.

"You are safe from her sting tonight. She claims exhaustion from her journey and is taking a tray in her room," he explained. And a footman, he added mentally, or a pair of them. Spending his money recklessly always seemed to whet her other appetites. God help them all.

Olympia's sigh of relief was quite telling. "I take it you spent some time with my aunt today?" he asked

She didn't precisely roll her eyes in response, but the temptation to do so was upon her. He could see it.

"I greeted her in the drawing room upon her return, as Mrs. Webster kindly pointed out that it was now my duty to do so. The embroidery I despise was actually less painful."

"Then why do it?" he asked. "The embroidery, that is. The other bit I understand. Mrs. Webster says to jump and we all jump."

"Because it is expected," Olympia replied. "In order to meet the standards society has set for me, I must prick my fingers until they are sore and blistering. But alas, this morning, I think Lady Florence inflicted more pain than my own clumsiness with a needle."

"The dower house is uninhabitable at the moment, and the work that it needs cannot be completed until spring," Griffin offered. "But there are other options. I have no issue with sending her away. She likes Liverpool well enough and when the weather has cleared, she can return there."

"You may not have issue with it, but I daresay she will. And I would not let her out of my sight, were I you. Turning your back on a woman such as she is ill advised at best."

Griffin did not respond to that, but he was impressed that she'd taken Florence's measure so quickly. If only his uncle had not been blinded by her beauty. Deciding a change of subject was in order, he turned to her. "I should not say this," he said, turning to face her. Every detail of her appearance, from the simply styled wealth of dark hair to the cut of her scarlet gown and all the attributes it displayed so charmingly lured him. He also noted the blush that stained her cheeks as his gaze traveled over her.

"In truth," he continued, "I should feel guilty to possess such feelings... but I am glad you are here. Whatever Mr. Swindon was thinking when he completely ignored my requirements, I can honestly say that I am glad that you have made your way here to Darkwood Hall... and to me."

Her blush deepened, but rather than acknowledge what he'd said and what it might possibly mean, she asked, "And what were your requirements, precisely? I know you were seeking a spinster... but that is a very strange type of woman to seek, don't you think?"

CHAPTER TEN

THERE WERE things he had to tell her, things that could possibly effect her decision to remain. He dreaded it, outlining their lonely future together for her. But it had to be done. He wouldn't have her stay on a lie.

Griffin waved the footmen away and helped her to her seat himself. When they were out of earshot, he spoke softly. "I have chosen, for reasons I will not discuss, not to have children. The Griffin line will end with me. The estates and title will pass to a distant cousin. For that reason, I wanted a woman who had given up the notion of children."

Another servant entered, prepared to serve the soup, and Olympia paused before answering until they'd gone again. Griffin was only too well aware that nothing he said to her within hearing of any of the servants would be private. They strained to take in every word simply to report it to Mrs.

Webster or to Lady Florence, depending on how and where their loyalties lay.

When the servants had all retreated, she pressed him again. "It doesn't bother you that all of what you've worked for will just be handed to some distant and possibly undeserving relative?"

Griffin shrugged. It was of little consequence whether it bothered him or not. If she knew the truth, if he was free to tell her the truth, she would understand that the risk of bringing a child into the hell of his life was simply too much. "I question on a daily basis whether or not I am deserving of this... my cousins, John and Alfred, were well prepared to take on the running of this estate. I was content to live in the dower house with my work. I have, for the longest time, focused more on plants than people... to the point I often have no notion of how to get on with them."

"That is a skill that can be learned. Clearly you have some natural ability in dealing with difficult people as you have not yet murdered Mrs. Webster or sacked her without a reference. I can't imagine a person any harder to get on with," she replied cheekily.

Laughing would only encourage her, so he refrained, but his lips quirked with amusement regardless. "She is difficult," he admitted. "But she has devoted herself to this family and to Darkwood Hall. Under the circumstances, she's earned a bit of leeway."

"A bit," she agreed. "Not enough to be positively rebellious and rude to her employers."

"I've spoken with her. She understands my position... and yours. Things will improve."

Olympia pressed on. "And if they do not?"

"Then I will speak to her again. Is there some other topic we can discuss? Something less likely to result in bitter disagreement?"

How SHE WANTED to press him further, to demand to know what power that woman wielded within the walls of Darkwood Hall! But he'd made it abundantly clear that he found the topic tiresome. If she continued, he'd come to find her tiresome, as well.

Electing to change the subject, she said, "I know you were reluctant for me to go into the village, but my wardrobe is sadly lacking, especially this far north."

His gaze was shuttered when he replied. "Liverpool would be a better option. The village is very small and very limited, but I won't be going there again for several weeks."

He wanted to keep her from the village and whatever gossip might abound there, she could tell. Was it to protect her or was it to protect his own interests? "Limited options are fine so long as they are warm. I only need to obtain fabric. My maid is skilled enough to produce the garments herself. You don't mind if I go into the village do you? So long as I take a servant with me?" Olympia knew that he would not be able to refuse, since those were the very conditions he'd laid down earlier that day.

His heavy sigh was answer enough. "Certainly, you should go into the village... But I must warn you, they will not be welcoming."

"But you cannot tell me why?"

His visage grew dark. The spark of anger in his eyes was quick and fierce. "Because they are superstitious fools with small minds and small lives. They've nothing better to do than gossip about things they know naught of."

The remainder of the dinner passed benignly. He talked of the distant history of Darkwood Hall, but did not speak of more recent events. It was very telling. Whatever tragedy or darkness had befallen the house, it had been recent enough that the villagers still spoke of it, and recent enough that the current Lord was uncomfortable with her knowing about it.

When the meal had ended, Olympia rose and he did as well. "Would you join me in the library? There are things we should discuss privately."

Like the consummation of their marriage, Olympia realized. Part of her was scandalized and horrifically embarrassed. Another part of her was eager to learn more, to finally have the gaps in her knowledge filled. She wasn't totally ignorant, after all, but what little she did know couldn't possibly be all of it. Surely what she'd learned from eavesdropping on the whispered conversations of scullery maids was not all there was to it?

Allowing Griffin to lead her to the room in question, she barely stifled a gasp when she entered the wondrous chamber. Shelves upon shelves were filled to overflowing with leather bound tomes. Her fingers itched to trace the spines of those books, to peruse them at leisure, to lose herself within the pages.

"You are an avid reader, I take it?" he asked.

"I was," she said, drifting toward one of the bookshelves. Idly, she caressed the books, tracing the intricately tooled leather. It had been ages since she'd had free access to so many books. Her uncle had disapproved of reading for women, thinking their brains too feeble to accommodate such a wealth of information. Olympia shuddered as she recalled the last time he'd caught her in their library. He'd dragged her from the room by her hair, locked her in her chamber for days with naught but bread and water for being defiant. But she wouldn't tell her husband that. He would ask more questions and then the whole sordid and ugly affair would come out.

"After my parents passed away," she continued, "And my aunt and uncle took over our home, I was no longer permitted to read. Or if I was, my chores took so much of my time that reading was simply impossible. But alas, my uncle felt that books would lead to impure thoughts," she replied, her voice soft and reverent.

"Do they?"

She glanced back at him then, dropping her hands from the books she was fondling. "That depends entirely upon the book, now doesn't it?"

His gaze was direct and impossibly hot. It was also focused on her lips in a way that said only too clearly he was recalling their one kiss. She'd been able to think of little else, herself.

"To be honest and rather blunt," he finally said, "I am in favor of impure thoughts. In fact, impure thoughts are precisely what I wished to discuss with you."

Her heart began to race. "You are very bold with such proclamations for a man who never intended to have more than a marriage in name only."

He leaned against the large desk, crossed his legs at the ankles and his arms over his chest. The stance made her aware of just how large he was, how the fabric of his coat strained over the heavy muscles of his arms and the bulging of his thighs brought to mind the way he'd looked when she'd first seen him astride that wicked stallion.

"I am bold... but you are not ready for our marriage to be a true union yet. There are things that I want from you, to do with you, that would shock you, Olympia... and while a little shock can be a good thing, I would rather introduce you to carnal matters more slowly. I want all of this to be a pleasurable experience for you and like so many good things, it's always sweeter when you've waited for it.""

What things? The question popped unbidden to her

mind, but she managed to just refrain from asking it aloud. Surely the answer would make very little sense to her and the embarrassment of the topic was more than she could bear. And the longer they waited, she realized, the more tense and difficult things between them would become. It was as if the Sword of Damocles was hanging over her head, ready to drop at any minute. She'd welcome it just to have the uncertainty at an end.

And she had to admit to far more practical and more mercenary reasons, though it pained her to do so. Until their marriage was consummated, he could still send her away and seek an annulment. Until they were one, her position would remain unsecured and the possibility of returning to her aunt and uncle loomed over her.

Having that thought brought home the uncomfortable reality of just how desperate her situation was. So, she spoke as matter-of-factly as possible and tried to still the telling tremors in her voice.

"I have had more time to accustom myself to the idea of consummating our union than many brides." Her tone was far more firm than she actually felt. "It wasn't until I arrived here that I was informed you did not intend for ours to be a true marriage... During the journey here, I had quite a bit of time to consider the matter."

He grinned. "And what conclusions did you reach, wife?"

Olympia looked away, unable to meet his gaze as she spoke. "That my ignorance is an impediment, and the longer I remain in ignorance the greater my fears and doubts will become."

"We shall endeavor to resolve your ignorance, but I will not come to your bed tonight," he said.

Olympia let out a breath she hadn't even been aware she was holding. It was equal parts relief and disappointment. "I don't understand."

He shoved away from the desk and stalked toward her, only stopping when they were toe to toe. She was forced to tip her head back to be able to look at him as he spoke.

"When I come to your bed, it will not be about duty, or about submitting to your husband the way a wife should... when I come to your bed, Olympia, it will be because you wish for me to be there—because you need me to be there. It will be because I have done what a man ought to when he means to make a woman his lover."

"And what, pray tell, is that?" she asked.

"I will have awakened you to passion...Slowly, reverently, and with all the skill that I possess. Desire, Olympia, is not something to be rushed, but rather is something to be fed over time, to be tended until it is lush and ripe."

There was no time to think or even process what he'd just said to her. He swooped in, his lips settling over hers in such a proprietary manner that she could do nothing but submit. And savor.

Heat built within her, slow and steady. A soft languor settled into her body and forced her to simply sink against him. And then came the satisfaction when his arms closed about her, tightening until she was pressed completely against him. There was a strange choreography to what was happening between them, a give and take that allowed her to feel, even in her ignorance, that she was not entirely power-less. Every movement, every sound elicited a response from him. It was a heady feeling.

The hardness of his body was a wonder to her, the firm press of his chest and his granite-like thighs. But there was something else, the hard and insistent ridge of his sex as it pressed against her belly.

Yes, she was innocent, and there was much she did not know. But that was unmistakable. Suddenly she was no longer standing on her own two feet. Instead, he'd born her back against the bookshelves, lifting her until his thighs were nestled between her own. The hardness of him pressed between her thighs, and even through the layers of fabric that separated them, it was insistent, bold, and it beckoned to a part of her she'd never before recognized—an inner wanton that had been silent to that point.

The kiss deepened, his tongue delving between her lips, sliding against hers in a way that shocked her. She had not thought to like it, but more than that, she was not prepared for the immediate craving for more. The taste of him was intoxicating. The feelings he invoked in her were beyond anything she'd ever experienced—heady, volatile. She felt reckless and bold. It was that which prompted her to kiss him back, to meet his questing tongue stroke for maddening stroke.

Kissing, she soon realized, involved more than just the meeting of lips. It was the soft, slow stroke of his tongue, the sting of his teeth as he bit her lower lip. And there was a rhythm to it. Slow and easy would give way to fast and consuming. Soft touches would be replaced with demanding ones only to recede into gentleness again. She felt dizzy from it all, swept away into a realm where little mattered beyond the touch of his mouth to hers, the weight of his body against her, and the pressure of his hands as they tightened on her hips, drawing her even closer.

Abruptly, he pulled back from her. His breath was a harsh rasp against her ear. He pressed his forehead to hers, apparently reluctant to let her go entirely.

"Did I do something wrong?" she asked, bereft at the sudden loss.

"No. You did everything right... but I meant what I said, Olympia. This will not be rushed, and if I were to allow this to continue right now, I would not be able to help myself."

She wanted to ask him to stay, to ask him to continue, to tell him that she wanted him to join her in her bed, but her earlier boldness had fled. He settled her back on the floor and turned away. Before she could even speak to call him back, he was gone. She stood alone in the library, listening to the sound of his retreating footsteps as they echoed the hammering of her own heart.

CHAPTER ELEVEN

GRIFFIN HAD LEFT Olympia in the library more than an hour ago, retreating to his work room in the conservatory to produce more of the elixir he'd developed for Cassandra. He'd made some slight changes to the formula, small adjustments to the amount of lavender and verbena, while adding chamomile for its soothing effect. He struggled to put his bride from his mind as he bypassed the door to his own chamber and strode toward the end of the corridor. When it forked, he turned to his left and toward the locked door that held all of Darkwood Hall's secrets at bay. There were only two keys to the door. He held one and Mrs. Webster held the other.

Slipping it from the pocket of his waistcoat, he fitted it into the lock and turned it slowly. The sound of metal grating against metal was impossibly loud in the darkened hall, but there was no one about to hear it. The servants were abed, as was Olympia.

The door swung inward and he stepped inside, closing it quickly behind him and relocking it. There was a small table just inside the door that bore a candle and tinderbox. Lighting the candle quickly, he moved on, traversing the corridor with an ease that came only from frequency. Near the end was another flight of stairs. He took them up and into the small turret room.

It held nothing but a simple mattress in the middle of the room. The windows were covered with bars. A girl sat on the floor before them, looking up at the moon that shone through as she wailed softly.

"Cassandra," he said softly. "It's me. Griffin. Can you hear me?"

There was no response. He'd been speaking to her thus, every night, for more than a decade. She had yet to respond intelligibly. There were some nights, such as the present, where she simply ignored him altogether. No, he thought. Not ignored. That implied she was choosing not to speak to him. In her present state, she had not awareness that he was even present. She was locked so deeply in her own mind that nothing outside of her own insanity even existed.

But there were other nights, nights where she was vicious and cruel. Nights that, if she could have reached him, she would have torn his throat out with her bare hands.

As he often did, Griffin sat on the floor. She moved then,

rocking slightly. And the leather straps at her ankles and wrists, fastened with metal rings that would attach to chains to bind her when she was too violent to be free, clinked loudly in the nearly silent room. They were a necessary evil at times. Without them, she would have killed Mrs. Webster, or him, or herself. For the time being, she was free to roam the confines of her room if she chose, but only to a point. She was restrained with a heavily padded belt looped with a chain that allowed for a safe zone so to speak, where they could enter the room and be out of her reach, where they could safely observe her.

"You were very sad last night," he remarked. "I could hear you crying. So could Olympia."

She cocked her head then, intrigued by the sound of a new word. Her lips moved, almost as if she were trying to repeat the string of syllables. But she had not spoken in years.

"I've married her," he said. "She's lovely. I wish you could know her... and that she could know you. One day, Cassie, you will be well. Whatever has happened to destroy your mind will be reversed and you will be free of all this."

She looked at him then, turning back to glance over her shoulder as she hunched forward. It was not the posture of a woman. It was the posture of a wild animal—a threatened one. It was also the only warning he had. She launched herself at him, teeth and claws. One of her hands connected with his cheek, scoring his flesh.

He backed away slowly as she screeched, tugging at her

bonds as she tried to reach him with hands already bloodied from her incessant scratching of the floor. That he was just out of reach only infuriated her more. She began to tug at her hair, pulling at it so viciously that it began to come out in her hands.

Griffin stepped forward then, ducking until he could grab her from behind. Wrestling her to the floor, his arms locked about her, he held her as tightly as he could without injuring her further. And then he rocked her gently, lulling her.

Mrs. Webster entered the room. She spoke softly, as she only ever did in Cassandra's presence. "The whole house is awake now. The new footmen are whispering about banshees."

"I'd rather it were banshees," he admitted gruffly.

"It isn't because of you," the woman offered brusquely. "It's because of all *he* did to her. Tormented the wee thing till her poor mind just broke under the strain."

"I don't wish to discuss it," he said sharply.

"Whether we discuss it or not, it's still the truth! And you've brought a young and lovely bride into this house. How long before you're on her the same way he was on every woman who crossed this threshold?"

Fury welled within him. "I am not my uncle."

"And your father?" Mrs. Webster asked. "He wasn't so much better, now was he? Knowing what this family is, the curse that follows it, put two children in your mother's belly and then a bullet in his own head!"

"Enough!" Griffin shouted so loudly that the room nearly shook with it. Dust drifted down from the rafters. In his arms, Cassandra screamed louder. "Do not speak of my parents again. And you will not mention my uncle in this room ever. Are we clear?"

Mrs. Webster nodded. "Very well, my lord. But you shouldn't come in here alone. She fears men, you see. Even those that would do her no harm. If you must come to see her, wait until I can come with you."

The truth of that burned to his very soul. Cassandra did fear him. Slowly, being as gentle with her as possible, he lowered her to the floor and rose. He walked away from her slowly, reluctantly and filled with the same guilt and regret that always consumed him. He had failed to protect her and she was paying the ultimate price for it. Trapped in her own mind, in a world where unspeakable things were visited on her over and over again, there was no reprieve.

"I thought to comfort her when I heard her cries," he said softly. "But it appears you are right and I have only made it worse."

"Sometimes, I think your presence is a comfort to her. On her good days, that is. But on her bad days, when she wails and carries on in the daytime, too, when not a soul has spoken to her, it is not. Yet you come here every night, you talk to her, and then you blame yourself when she does this."

"I think I'm making her worse," he admitted.

"No. But you're not making her better... and maybe it's

time to accept that there won't *be* a better for her. Some things, once broken, cannot be put back together."

Cassandra had ceased her rocking back and forth, but she was still on alert, her eyes wide and shifting quickly between them. "You're in a shockingly charitable mood tonight, Mrs. Webster. Almost comforting even."

The housekeeper shrugged. "I'm not without feeling, my lord. But that doesn't mean I approve of how you've handled things. There are hospitals for people like Cassandra. And I think it's high time you looked into one."

"I can't do that," he said firmly.

"Why not?"

He glanced at her. "Because it's my fault she's here... like this. And it's my responsibility to care for her."

"She was broken when she was born, my lord, and because she was broken, she was an easy target for those that would harm her. It turned something inside her... made her vicious and cruel—savage. I remember how your mother cried when she killed that little dog... when she lashed out at the servants. You did not see it because you were away at school."

"And while I was away at school, laughing and playing with my friends, she was at his mercy!" he said stiffly. He looked back at Cassandra, crouched on the floor, her hair in wild disarray and her eyes wide with a kind of fear he had never known. "I failed her once, Mrs. Webster. Whatever it takes, I will not fail her again," he said emphatically. "Bring me the new mixture. We'll get enough of it in her that she will sleep tonight."

The woman approached cautiously, keeping a wary eye on the young woman in his arms. Together they forced her mouth open and poured a small amount of the sedative in her. Mrs. Webster rubbed her throat to coax her to swallow.

The housekeeper sat down with her then, taking the half wild young woman into her arms and rocking her like an infant. It never ceased to amaze him that a woman so cold and vicious to others could be so tender with his sister. Still puzzling over that fact, Griffin left the room, but couldn't shake the heavy yoke of guilt that seemed to be growing heavier by the day.

IN HER ROOM, Olympia had poured over the contents of the letters. They were difficult to read, the ink faded with time and often smeared from what she assumed were tears. With what Griffin had said to her in the library and with certain things explained in graphic detail in those letters, she now had a better idea of what he meant. It did shock her, but it also excited her. But it was the journal that proved more interesting reading.

She was nearly halfway through the book before she realized precisely who Patrice Landon was. The woman who'd been written to so passionately and who had clearly been so

well loved was Griffin's mother. As she neared the end of the
journal, with Patrice outlining the discovery of her preg-
nancy, Olympia wondered if the unborn child she spoke of
was actually Griffin.

As the night wore on, the crying began. Olympia closed
the book and listened to the wailing that reverberated down
the darkened halls. He'd made promises, offered reassurances
that nothing untoward was occurring in the house. But the
sounds she'd heard made that nearly impossible to believe.

Only untold suffering could result in a human being
producing such agonizing cries. She couldn't ignore it,
couldn't pretend it wasn't happening. Rushing toward her
door, she flung it open and rushed out into the hallway,
smacking directly into the broad and immovable chest of her
husband.

"You should be in bed," he chided softly.

Stepping back, Olympia looked up at him. The light
spilling from her room illuminated his face and the bloody
scratch that marred his cheek. Reaching up, she touched it
with her fingertips and he winced.

"It is impossible to sleep in a house where one clearly
suffers so much. Who is she, Griffin? Who is it that wails so in
the night?"

"At one time, she was my sister," he said.

"She is no longer your sister, then?" she asked, puzzled by
his answer.

He looked away from her as he answered, and his voice

was thick with emotion. "If there is aught left inside her of my sister, it is buried so deep that I doubt I will ever reach it again... but I will continue to try. To do less would be a disservice to her and to our parents."

There was such pain in his voice, such guilt and remorse that Olympia was overwhelmed. She thought of the journals and letters in her room, things she'd essentially stolen from him. If she offered them to him, would they give him peace, make him feel less alone? Or would it simply reopen old wounds?

Uncertain of what else to do and possessing no other way to convey her sorrow for him, she stepped closer and closed her arms about him. "I would help you if I could."

His hand curled around the fall of her braid, tugging her head back until their gazes locked. "You have helped me. More than you know... Go back to your bed, Olympia, while I have the strength to let you occupy it alone."

CHAPTER TWELVE

Accompanied by a footman and Collins, Olympia made her way along the main thoroughfare of the village. The snow had not amounted to much, but the temperatures were cold enough for the ground to be frozen solid rather than the soggy, muddy mess that they'd first arrived in.

The village of Easton on Ryburn was small, incredibly so, as Griffin had warned her. Still, there was a milliner, a haber-dasher and a linen draper all within a short distance of one another. It would be a quick trip for them, she thought.

"You may wait out here," she told the footman.

"But, m'lady, I was instructed not to let you out of me sight," he said, his voice panicky and high pitched.

"And she won't be out of your sight. There are windows right here where you can watch her the entire time we're in the shop," Collins said impatiently. "Your job will be complete and her ladyship can order personal items without either of you dying of the humiliation."

The young footman blushed and then nodded furiously. "Yes, Miss Collins! M'lady?"

"That will be perfectly fine, Thomas," Olympia agreed as she tried to make sense of Collins. As a scullery maid, she'd been meek and quite timid. With her elevated station, she'd become quite a force to contend with. Still, referring to the purchase of unmentionables in front of the footman was hardly appropriate.

Of course, her patience for Collins was also challenged by her lack of sleep. She'd lain awake for the better part of the night thinking of Griffin and his confession in the hallway. Had he not been so distraught he would not have told her about his sister. She was certain of it. But he had, and now she could not put it from her mind. Nor could she put the journal and those letters from her mind, and all she'd learned of his parents and the passion they'd shared. It all pressed heavily upon her and she wondered what course of action to take. To tell him and damn the consequences, or to keep the secret and let it fester inside her?

Entering the shop, Collins at her heels, the few women gathered inside immediately fell silent. The hush that swept through the shop was immediate and the atmosphere palpably tense. Ignoring the curious stares and those that bordered on hostile, Olympia approached the shopkeeper.

"We are in need cloth for day dresses... wool, preferably, something warm. And velvets for dinner dresses, I think."

"You'll need to go to Liverpool, my lady," the shopkeeper said. "We don't have anything here for you."

Olympia looked at the table to her left, piled high with bolts of wool in an array of colors. "Are these not suitable for me, then? Are the colors unflattering to me perhaps?"

The woman's ruddy complexion deepened with either anger or embarrassment, or perhaps both. "You'd be happier with the finer fabrics available to you there, Lady Darke."

Olympia's smile did not waiver, though her eyes were cool and hard as she stared the woman down. "No doubt I would be, but Liverpool is a journey I am unprepared to make today. And I need several lengths of wool... enough to complete at least three day dresses. I like the green, don't you? I think it would look lovely on me."

"It would indeed, my lady," one of the other women in the shop spoke up. Her voice was thin and high, tremulous as though she were terrified to even speak up. "I have one in the same fabric, but it would be much finer on you, I'm certain."

Given that one of her other customers had shown support, the shopkeeper was left with no other option but to assist her. Clearly, it was against her will, as the woman bristled visibly as she began collecting the bolts of cloth.

"The blue, as well," Olympia added, pointing to a bolt dangerously close to the bottom of the pile. "And the pink. Those should do nicely for now."

"Yes, m'lady," the shopkeeper ground out from between clenched teeth.

Olympia turned her attention to the woman who had spoken up. She was tall and rail thin, her blonde hair swept back into a lovely cascade of soft curls. She had a delicate quality about her, fae-like, in spite of her impressive height. "Thank you so much for your assistance. May I have your name please?"

"Elizabeth Marsters, Lady Darke," the woman answered. "Forgive me, but I cannot stay. I must get home quickly."

The woman was gone in an instant. Another woman in the shop spoke up then. "Don't mind her, dear! It's a bit much being confronted with the woman who has the title meant for you!"

"I beg your pardon?" Olympia asked, not certain she'd heard the woman correctly.

"Miss Elizabeth was quite close to the eldest son of the late Lord Darke... It was common knowledge he meant to ask for her. But then the tragedy occurred," the woman said, dropping her voice to a low whisper that managed to be everything but discreet. "But, of course, you know all about that."

The last was uttered in a smug way, as if the woman fully well knew that Olympia was being kept in ignorance. But she wouldn't admit it, not to her, even if it meant her ignorance continued for far longer. "My husband has spoken of it," she said. It wasn't precisely a lie.

"I'm sure he has. Such a shame," the woman continued. "You made an excellent choice."

"The green?" Olympia asked. "I do hope it will be flattering."

The woman laughed. "That too, my dear, but I meant in husbands. Fine looking man, rich as Croesus, and if the luck of the Lords Darke holds true, not long for this world to plague you."

Olympia was still gaping after the woman as the bell of the door tinkled from her exit.

"I'd say she won that round," Collins intoned solemnly.

"Be quiet, Collins. Or you may be begging her for work."

"Yes, m'lady."

"I'm only teasing, Collins," Olympia said. "We're in this together, you and I?"

The maid nodded but then flushed guiltily. "Yes, m'lady. There's something I need to tell you, but I don't think to I ought to say it here."

"Then tell me in the carriage on the way home. We'll be private enough there."

"Yes, ma'am."

After choosing several lengths of fabric for gowns, Olympia chose muslins and linens for undergarments. Her own were sadly worn. With arrangements made for their order to be delivered to Darkwood Hall, they left the shop.

The experience was eerily similar to the first. The shop-keeper was rude. The other shoppers were clearly nonplussed by her presence. Brazening it out, Olympia found herself exhausted by the whole debacle. As they left, she knew there was one more stop that had to be made. As the new Lady Darke, it was her duty to inquire at the church and see what the community's needs were. She could only hope the vicar would be more welcoming than everyone else had been.

As they walked toward the church, which was at the heart of the village, people crossed the street to avoid her. Others simply turned their backs. Whatever had happened at Darkwood Hall, it wasn't simply a tragedy. It was also a scandal. While she despised gossip, not knowing would only make her life more difficult and would make it increasingly hard to fulfill her duties.

Having a purpose in her life was vitally important to her. She'd realized it more so of late than ever before. While her parents had not been wealthy, they'd always encouraged charity and good works. Much of her time as a younger woman had been devoted to helping the poor and the sick, but when her parents had passed and her Aunt and Uncle had taken over their home, they'd dismissed most of the servants and instead used her for labor. She didn't mind the work, but it was unnecessary. Her parents had left more than enough money to see to her care, and yet she'd been subjected to a life of penury, working in the kitchens as a servant rather than living there as a respected daughter of the house.

It wasn't so different from the activities she'd engaged in

while helping to feed hungry children at the church they'd attended. It was the blow to her pride that had been truly damaging. But that was all in the past now and she was once again in a position to do good works. Helping others had been incredibly satisfying. She'd looked forward to that with the change in her station— feeling useful again rather than simply used.

"I must speak with the vicar, Collins. You may wait with the carriage if you like."

Collins nodded. "Certainly, m'lady."

It was clear that Collins was immediately relieved at not having to accompany her into the church. Recalling the pious and drunken ramblings of her uncle, she found she couldn't blame her. Where she'd once enjoyed attending church herself, it no longer held any appeal for her after being browbeaten with religion for so long, especially by a man who could not have been a greater hypocrite.

Entering the church, she found the vicar sorting through hymnals. The church itself was modest, but still lovely and clearly built with the ancient gothic cathedrals in mind. It mimicked them but on a far less grand scale.

"Good afternoon," the vicar called out jovially. "How may I help you?"

"I've actually come to ask that question myself," Olympia offered with a smile. "I am Olympia, Lady Albus Griffin, Viscountess Darke."

The vicar's warm smile faded. While he didn't exactly

appear unwelcoming, he was concerned, guarded. "What sort of assistance would you offer, Lady Darke?"

Olympia considered her answer carefully. "I was rather hoping that you might be able to tell me what is needed here? I volunteered with many charities while I was in London and was hoping that I might find some sort of purpose in helping those less fortunate here in my new home parish."

The vicar frowned thoughtfully. "I apologize for speaking so bluntly, your ladyship, but I fear that very few people in the area would welcome your assistance. The name of Darke is not well received."

"I have gleaned that from my interactions thus far." Deciding to beard the lion in its den, she asked the question directly. "And why is that precisely?"

His expression had been thoughtful before, but at that point, his gaze shuttered and any hint of welcome faded. "I couldn't say, m'lady."

"You cannot say is not the same as saying you do not know," she pointed out.

"Regardless of whether I am simply unwilling or inno-cently ignorant, I have no intention of discussing the matter further. If you have questions about the history with the Lords Darke and the villagers, I suggest you take them to your husband."

And she was back to the beginning, she thought bitterly. Everyone wanted to whisper and point fingers, but no one would tell her anything worth knowing.

"If you think of any way that I might be of service within the parish, please let me know," she reiterated. "Obviously, you'll know where to reach me."

"Yes, my lady," he said. "Good day, my lady."

The dismissal was quite firm. It was a first for her, being tossed out of a church on her ear. Turning on her heel, she left with her head held high though it goaded her to do so. There was only one solution. Griffin would have to tell her. Whether he liked it or not, she would not continue to blunder about in ignorance. It was long past time he told her the entire truth.

Retreating to the carriage, she found Collins offering sweetly flirtatious smiles to the footman who appeared to be equally enamored of her. That was quite a turnabout. "Collins, we're going home. Now, please."

"Yes, my lady."

"Lady Darke! Lady Darke!"

Olympia turned back to see a shopkeeper running towards her.

Breathless, the man stopped a few feet away from her. "These came on the mail coach! Wanted to save me boy a trip to Darkwood Hall."

Olympia accepted the packet of letters from him. "Thank you, sir. What is your name?"

"John Short, m'lady. My wife and I run the mercantile, and our son does deliveries."

"And you are also the local postmaster?" she asked.

He flushed. "No, m'lady. The local postmaster refused to hold mail for his lordship after what happened... so I do it."

"I see... Are there other merchants in town who have refused to do business with his lordship?"

"Most of 'em, m'lady. But I reckon he's never been nothing but kind to me," the man replied stoutly.

"Thank you, Mr. Short. What sort of items do you sell in your Mercantile?"

"Bit o'this, bit o'that, m'lady."

"Fabric and sewing notions?"

"Only a bit. Nothing so fine as would befit a lady of your station."

Olympia smiled at that. Before the small bit of coin Swindon had provided her, her wardrobe had consisted of only two dresses and one of them had been worn until it was little better than a rag. "Collins, go cancel the order with the milliner, the linen draper and the haberdasher. We'll purchase what we need from Mr. Short, and if he does not have it, he will order it for us. Won't you, Mr. Short?"

The man's flush deepened but his chest puffed up with pride. "I certainly will, m'lady. You'll always be welcome in our store."

"Take me to it now, if you please Mr. Short," she said. "I am in the mood to shop."

While the selection of fabrics was smaller, she found several that were suitable. The buttons and other items were more plain and serviceable, but Olympia took no exception to that. With her shopping complete, she and Collins returned to the carriage.

"Collins, what was it you wished to speak to me about?" Olympia asked, recalling the maid's earlier statement.

Collins ducked her head. "I overheard a conversation, m'lady, while I was in your dressing room. It backs up to his lordship's dressing room and I suppose his chamber as well."

"Yes... what did you hear?"

"I couldn't make it all out, but it seems as if, the other Viscountess that was, Lady Florence, had been betrothed to him at one time."

"I think you misheard, Collins... But I will look into the matter."

The maid nodded, but her expression remained grim, prompting Olympia to wonder if she had the whole truth.

On the short journey back to Darkwood Hall, Olympia steeled herself for the confrontation to come. She needed the truth from him now, whether he wished to share it or not.

CHAPTER THIRTEEN

OLYMPIA ENTERED the drawing room upon her return, unwilling to be imprisoned in her room again for the remainder of the day. Hiding from Lady Florence was hardly a long term solution to her situation.

No sooner had she thought the name than the woman entered, sweeping into the room wearing an elaborately embroidered day dress in soft shade of violet. Her hair was arranged in a confection of curls that looked as if one loosened pin would send the lot of tumbling down her back.

"Oh, you've been shopping, I hear!" she cooed. "The village is rather disappointing... not to mention very *grim*. You should accompany me to Liverpool. I have a wonderful dressmaker there, and she makes the naughtiest little underthings." Lady Florence stopped and then giggled. "But I don't suppose you'll be needing those. I understand Griffin is quite reluctant to cement your marriage."

How would she know that? *Mrs. Webster, of course.* "You're quite interested in the goings on within our chambers... And yet I hear there is an endless stream of footman lined up at your chamber door."

Lady Florence shrugged elegantly. "Not an endless stream...two or three that I dally with when the fancy strikes. You will too, one day. Having lovers, Lady Darke, is infinitely preferable to having husbands. And when Griffin inevitably succumbs to the curse that befalls all men of this family, you'll understand precisely why that is. The name Darke is quite fitting... for they are that. Black to their souls."

Olympia shivered. He'd said the night before that the weeping woman had once been his sister but that if there was aught left of her it was buried beyond his reach. Was this the same kind of affliction that Lady Florence spoke of? Would he become like Cassandra, a violent and wounded creature lashing out at those around her? Screaming in the night?

"You are certainly a doomsayer, Lady Florence," Olympia said, regaining her composure and schooling her features into a neutral mask. "My husband is quite sound and the picture of health."

Lady Florence laughed heartily. "Oh, he is! And so handsome, too! Did you know that it's illegal for me to marry a man who was my nephew by marriage? I checked. I thought perhaps that would be the perfect answer... but alas he turned me down flat, even when he desperately needed a bride to claim the inheritance left to him by that horrid old bat, Honoria. I thought it was just a convenient excuse, but he was actually telling the truth... Of course, it can still be arranged if one gets special dispensation from the bishop. And given that my marriage to Roger produced no children, and there is no blood relation between us, and that Griffin and I had a previous relationship—."

The conversation with Collins in the carriage came back to her then, along with a feeling of dread. "What previous relationship?"

Lady Florence smiled. "We've known each other for ages, you see."

"What is your point, Lady Florence? You try my patience!"

She rose then and walked over to where Olympia stood, leaning in to whisper next to her ear. "He turned down my offer of marriage... but that's all he rejected, Lady Darke. Did you really think a man as virile as Griffin would exist in this isolated place without any feminine comfort? He's been my lover for years. Enjoy it when he comes to your chamber. I fully intend to enjoy it when he returns to mine!"

It couldn't possibly be true, Olympia thought. But as Lady Florence smiled at her, she knew that it must be. The woman was too beautiful by far. Lovelier than any she'd ever seen. Why else would he have turned her away in the library last night when she freely offered herself to him? Because his needs were being met elsewhere. The realization of it sank into her with the weight of stone. Had she been a fool to believe his words? Were his promises of a slow seduction merely an excuse to delay the dreaded act of being her lover?

"Good day, Lady Darke," Florence said and left the room in a swish of violet skirts.

Olympia sank onto the settee and tried to quell the sick feeling in her stomach. Had he truly been lovers with his uncle's wife? There was only one way to get an answer. She would simply have to confront her husband as she'd planned.

GRIFFIN HAD STRIPPED to his shirtsleeves as he worked. The small hothouse was kept at a steaming temperature for the survival of several rare plants that he'd cultivated in the hopes that their medicinal properties would provide some relief for Cassandra. And yet, he'd found nothing that worked.

Perhaps Mrs. Webster was right and it was time to give up. But the idea of placing her in an asylum, to be cared for by strangers, was something he could not bear. Of course there was also the brutal nature of their treatments. He couldn't allow that to happen to her if there was any other option. That he would continue to care for Cassandra as she had was the last promise he'd made to his mother before the fever took her.

Thinking of his parents, of the unfairness of their deaths —the dark days before his father had succumbed to madness and his mother's untimely death, his mood grew dark. And as he weighed the dilemma of his sister's affliction, Griffin felt darkness growing in him. The futile anger and the urge to lash out that always accompanied it were something that he tried desperately to keep at bay, but it times it proved too much for him.

With the last of the new cuttings repotted, he brushed off his hands, put away his tools and walked from the room. His father had loved horticulture, had believed adamantly that the cure for every illness could be found in nature. He'd schooled Griffin to continue his work, to keep searching for answers. There was no joy in it for him, however. Only duty. The plants his father had procured over the years, some purchased, some gifted to him, and yet others carefully carted home from the journeys he would take before his own condition had worsened were the only legacy he had left of the loving father he'd been.

Annoyed with his melancholy thoughts, Griffin left the conservatory, and the memories it stirred, behind him. His decision to put away his work for the day had naught to do with the fact that he was eager to see his bride, to find some excuse to have a few moments alone with her. A stolen kiss would improve his mood.

Climbing the stairs two at a time, he retreated to his chamber to wash up and don something that didn't leave him looking like a field hand. While Olympia appeared to be more than understanding about the informality and the unusual way in which his household was run, greeting her in his dirty shirtsleeves was hardly the best way to get on.

Stripping off his soiled shirt, Griffin poured water into the basin. It was cold, but he hadn't thought to have warm water sent up, so he would suffer it. He scrubbed his face vigorously and had just began to wash his chest when a soft knock sounded on the connecting door.

It would be Olympia, and it would be foolhardy to let her in. Stolen kisses were all well and good, but alone in the privacy of his chamber, he would want much more and he was not yet certain she was prepared for that.

He should speak to her through the closed door and then meet with her in the drawing room. If he meant to take his time in wooing her, establishing some sort of rapport with her before simply taking her to his bed, then entertaining her in his chamber was a temptation he could ill afford.

But where she was concerned, poor decisions were proving to be the rule rather than the exception. He crossed the room in long, quick strides and opened the door. It would shock her and part of him wanted to. He wanted to see her rattled by him in the same way that he was by her.

Taking in her expression, he watched her eyes widen, watched her tempting lips part then saw the stain of her blush creeping over her porcelain skin. She blinked several times, but in doing so, her eyes roved over him. He could feel her gaze on him like it was a weight. When she managed to turn her face away, she swallowed convulsively. She said nothing, but her actions told him all she needed to. She wanted him, whether she understood what that meant or not.

"Did you need something?" he asked. It was a subtle double entendre, one that would escape her entirely. But his own mind was supplying the answer for her. She needed him, and God help him, he needed her.

"I wanted to talk to you about some things that happened while I was in the village today," she said. "And also about some things that I have learned since Lady Florence has returned to Darkwood, but it can wait. I didn't realize you were—." She stopped abruptly as her mind failed to supply the words she needed.

"Undressed?" he offered helpfully.

"Indisposed," she corrected, using the more politely accepted term.

Griffin noted that, though she kept her gaze averted, he could see the pulse beating at the base of her throat. It fluttered wildly, a clear indication of just how unnerved she was by him and his current state of undress. "We are married, Olympia. The lack of a shirt should hardly keep you from saying whatever it is that you wish to say to me." His tone was casual, belying the fact that her nearness, the scent of her, incited a lust in him that he hadn't known himself capable of.

It went far beyond simply desire. It was a craving that burrowed into him, digging in with teeth and claws. There was something dark in it. Dark and ugly, but it was also insistent and would not be denied.

"Come in, Olympia, and speak your piece," he offered. It was a challenge and they both knew it.

CHAPTER FOURTEEN

OLYMPIA FELT THE PULL, the fire that burned just beneath her skin, raging and roaring to life every time she was in his presence. Desire, if that was truly what she was experiencing, was not the pleasant thing she'd read about in scandalous and forbidden poems. It was much darker, stronger, pressing in on her and driving her to behave in ways that she didn't understand. Even angry as she was, hurt and with her pitifully wounded pride, she still felt those stirrings of desire for him.

As she stepped over the threshold into his room, she knew that she was taking a step that was irrevocable and would alter *everything* in her life. She trembled slightly under the weight of that knowledge and of the questions about what was to come.

He didn't step back from her immediately, but stayed

near the door so that their bodies brushed as she moved past him. That simple touch created a hitch in her breath, raised gooseflesh on her skin and heightened her awareness of him to the point she could think of nothing else but the way he smelled, the way he had kissed her.

"You were correct when you said that I would not be well received in the village," she said, ignoring the fact that her voice sounded thin and tremulous. "Even the vicar was somewhat less than cordial."

He didn't smile, but his mouth did turn up at the corners in a slight quirk, his expression an odd mix of amusement and sadness. "I warned you. And what did our lovely villagers have to say about myself and Darkwood Hall?"

"Very little. Vague hints, misdirection and all flavored with an overarching sense of disdain and disapproval," she summarized. "Except for John Short. He and his wife were lovely. They also presented me with a packet letters. Swindon has written to you."

"I will answer it later," he replied. "I fear that this conversation may be more important."

Turning to face him directly, she forced her gaze upward to his face and ignored the distracting vision of the planes and ridges of his bare chest. "I must know what happened here, Griffin. It is an unfair thing to expect of me... that I should live in this house, under the stain of whatever occurred while being completely ignorant of any details."

He crossed his arms over his chest and lowered his head as if in deep in thought. It afforded her an opportunity to study him at leisure, to take in every detail of his form. The liquid heat that suffused her, that pooled in her belly, prompted her to take a step back from him. It wasn't him as much as it was the temptation he presented to her. She wanted him. While her knowledge of carnal matters was limited, it was sufficient to allow her to admit that. But it terrified her as much as it tempted her, because she understood the power of it.

Giving herself to him would be to give him a kind of power over her that she feared and craved. She wanted to know passion and desire. She wanted to know what it would be to lose herself entirely.

"My uncle was a violent man," he finally said. "He was always a violent man, lashing out at anyone near him. And in the last years of his life, he went quite mad... And his violence grew worse. In a fit of rage prompted by something none of us understand, he murdered both his sons."

Olympia gasped, her face going pale at the horror of what he disclosed. A small bench at the foot of his bed was the closest place to sit and she needed to. He'd called it a tragedy and it was, but it was also much worse than that. Sinking onto the bench, she clasped her hands in her lap so tightly that her knuckles went white. "When did this occur?"

"Less than a year ago," he stated simply. "In the dining room."

Horror blossomed inside her when she recalled their dinner the night before, sitting in a room that had witnessed such horrific violence from a father to his sons. "How can you bear to sit in that room?" she demanded.

He shrugged. "This house has seen many horrors over the years, Olympia. Were I to avoid every chamber or room that had witnessed violence I would have to sleep in the stables."

"What?"

His gaze was dark, his eyes cold and distant. "We're all mad, you see... Every man who has ever borne the title of Viscount Darke has gone quite mad. My uncle was not the first member of this family to commit atrocities against his relatives. But I mean to be certain he is the last... and that is why we will never have children, Olympia. That is why I mean to let the line die with me. There is something broken inside us that should not be passed on."

"How can you know that?" she demanded.

"I told you of my sister Cassandra, but what I did not tell you is that... she is afflicted with the same violent tendencies as my uncle. But unlike him, she is never sensible and just driven to fits of temper. She is like a wounded animal, lashing out viciously at anyone who comes near her. I would not visit that fate on anyone. And I would deny you children before I would condemn you to see any son or daughter you bore suffer in such a way."

"Madness can be caused by many things, Griffin! You

cannot be certain that any children we might have would be afflicted so!" she retorted.

"Certain? No, I cannot be certain. But it would be selfish to risk it. I will not do that, Olympia. I will not bring another person into this world to suffer the way my sister has... and while I display no symptoms now, there is no guarantee that years from now, or even months from now, will not succumb! My own father was fine for years, until one day he simply wasn't."

She rose then, frustrated by his answers, frustrated by things she did not understand. That frustration prompted her to pace as she considered how best to respond. "There are treatments—."

"And they are cruel and ineffective," he snapped. "You cannot understand the reality of what I have endured until you see it first hand."

Before Olympia could ask what he meant, he grabbed her by the arm and with his free hand, snagged a key that lay upon the mantle. She struggled to keep up with him as he stalked down the hallway toward the very door Mrs. Webster had barred her from entering. Once through it, he slowed somewhat, but the tension in him seemed to grow. Every muscle was taut and one ticked perceptibly in his jaw as he led her up a narrow flight of stairs.

The room was part of a turret or tower, the walls rounded and the windows heavily barred. But it was the girl in the center of the room that caught Olympia's eye. She looked like Griffin with her dark hair and eyes, but at the sight of them she shrieked like a banshee. The sound reverberated off the stone walls, the sound so chilling that Olympia could not stop herself from taking a step back.

When she did, Griffin turned on her. "You wanted to see. You wanted to understand," he reminded her in a fierce tone. "Well, now you have. This is my sister, Cassandra. We must keep her restrained to keep her from doing harm to others. At times, we must restrain her even further to keep her from doing harm to herself."

Olympia said nothing. She recognized that there was naught for her to say. He wasn't angry. Oh, his tone was sharp and his words could cut like a blade, but she'd seen it in his eyes when he looked at her. He was hurting. Griffin was in a kind of pain she couldn't fathom because he could not save someone he loved.

"She has torn at her skin until it is bloodied. Ripped handfuls of hair from her own head. No servants attend her. The last time I allowed a maid into this room, Cassandra nearly killed her," he said softly, turning away from her to take in the bloodied hands of his sister as she clawed at the floor.

Following his gaze, Olympia could see the bloodied, smeared fingerprints on the floor. "We could put down a rug for her. It might help."

He smiled, but it was not an expression of amusement. There was a wealth of sadness in that expression. "We tried. And she nearly suffocated herself with it... and selfish as I am, sometimes I even wish I'd found her a few moments later. Then her suffering and mine would be at an end."

CHAPTER FIFTEEN

OLYMPIA HAD no response for that, but none was required. While the statement had been uttered with conviction, it had also held a world of regret. But as she surveyed the broken woman before her, Olympia did not judge him for such a thought. If she'd had the misfortune to be in his present situation, she couldn't imagine that her own thoughts would be any different, or even as charitable.

"Oh Griffin, I'm so sorry," she said softly. "I can't imagine how awful this has been for you... for both of you."

"Mrs. Webster found my uncle and my cousins in the dining room," he continued. "She and I concealed the nature of their deaths as well as possible, laying the blame on a mysterious drifter who broke into the house intent on robbery."

"And people believed that? A drifter here in the middle of nowhere?"

He shook his head. "No. And that is why the people in the village are so reluctant to welcome you or anyone else from this house... they suspect that I am responsible. They believe that I killed my uncle and my cousins to gain the title. You are married to a man who could possibly go mad at any day and is already suspected of being a murderer."

"I know the truth... and even if you hadn't told me, I would never have believed that you were a murderer, Griffin," Olympia said firmly. "I cannot fathom the suffering you have known, that you have both endured and witnessed. But I am sorry for it."

At that moment, the girl began to shriek louder. She clawed at the restraints she wore, trying to reach them. Her teeth were bared and the violence of her actions was something that Olympia had never witnessed in her life. It was both terrifying and piteous. She was wounded and animalistic, broken inside in a way that can never be fixed.

"Our presence here distresses, her," Olympia said.

"At times. And at times she howls and rails whether she is alone or if I am present," he said. "But she may calm if we leave."

"Does Lady Florence know of her presence here?" Olympia asked as they moved toward the stairs.

"She does," Griffin replied, as he led her back to the main corridor. "But she cannot be bothered with Cassandra. She finds her presence here to be a nuisance when it disturbs her, but otherwise she never asks after her or even acknowledges her existence."

"She would use her to hurt you," Olympia stated firmly. "The woman is not to be trusted."

"No," he agreed. "She isn't. But at the same time, Florence will do nothing to harm me so long as she continues to have a generous allowance and the freedom to behave as scandalously as she chooses."

They left the tower room, heading down the stairs and back to his chamber. Olympia said nothing further until they were once again behind closed doors. Questions remained that had to be asked.

"Is she your lover?" she blurted out.

"What?" he demanded.

"Lady Florence... are you lovers?" she repeated.

"Where would you get such an idea?" His voice was heavy with suspicion.

Olympia noted that it was not an immediate denial but a misdirection. Pain stabbed at her and she recognized it for what it was. *Jealousy.*

"She's very beautiful. A woman such as her would be difficult to resist, I imagine," she said softly.

"Not so difficult," he said. "A lioness is beautiful, but I would not bed down with one. Florence is a beautiful facade hiding a rotting core. No, Olympia, she is not my lover."

Why would Lady Florence claim such a thing if there

were no truth to it? Olympia understood that she saw her as a threat, as an obstacle to what she wanted which was to remain in a position of power at Darkwood Hall. But such a thing could be easily verified or denied. Whether Griffin recognized it or not, Lady Florence was a force to be reckoned with. But then she examined his words carefully.

"Has she ever been your lover?" she asked.

His gaze grew shuttered, his expression hardening. "Olympia...," he paused then, sighed heavily. His head dropped to his chest and the offered up the dreaded words. "Yes. She was my lover."

"You engaged in an affair with your uncle's wife?"

He shook his head. "No. I brought my lover—my betrothed—here to meet my family before our wedding. And she became my uncle's lover and his wife instead of my own. Florence was my lover, but it was years ago... before she and my uncle married, before the depths of his illness became evident and long before I realized what fate likely lay in store for me."

She needed to sit, she realized. Her knees, already trembling, were about to fail her entirely. Relief, intense and overwhelming, assailed her. "I see," she finally managed. "I am sorry to have pressed you."

He paced the room, walking to the fireplace and back to the basin. Anger emanated from him and yet she did not feel threatened.

"I had warned Florence not to say anything to you of

this... I did not wish it known because I wanted to avoid any additional unpleasantness in this house. We've enough to contend with already!"

"I'm glad she said it... and I'm glad, though it pained you, that I asked you," Olympia confessed breathlessly. "If we are to be together, if this is to be a true marriage as you said, I would not have this secret between us."

"And what of your secrets, Olympia?" he asked. "What are you so very afraid of?"

"I don't understand what you mean," she lied.

Griffin approached her, kneeling before her where she sat. They were still not eye to eye, as he towered over her. She was forced to look up to meet his gaze, but they were so close she could see the tiny flecks of gold in the dark depths of his eyes and the faint glint of the few silver strands that shot through his black hair. His nearness made her heart race. It raised goose bumps on her flesh and caused a rush of liquid heat to pool between her thighs. Olympia blushed fiercely.

"You fear something. I can sense it in you. Is it me? Dark-wood Hall? What do you fear, Olympia?

"Nothing. I fear nothing, my lord—Griffin. It's simply that much has changed in my life and I am still growing accustomed to it all." It was a paltry excuse and she knew it.

He looked away from her, his expression pained. "If you wish to return to London—."

"No!" she said quickly, forcefully. There was nothing for her to go back to except pain and ruin. And while she'd only known him for a matter of days, she couldn't fathom letting go of the connection she felt with him. For the first time, in a very long time, she wanted something. It wasn't about survival or getting by or avoiding another's plans for her. She wanted him, whether it was for a night or forever.

"I want to be here with you," she said softly. "I want to be with you, Griffin." She wanted to say more, to explain in the plain words that he seemed to prefer that she wanted to be his wife in every way. But she lacked the courage to voice it. So instead, she leaned forward, so close that he could not mistake her invitation, and placed her hand on his cheek. The rasp of his whiskers against her palm made her shiver.

He clasped his hand over hers and brought it down, pressing it to his bare chest until she could feel his heartbeat thumping heavily beneath firm muscle and heated skin. Touching him so intimately, when she knew even greater intimacies were to come, had her swaying on her feet, unsteady and drunk with anticipation.

"There's no going back, Olympia. I need you to be very, very sure," he warned softly, his voice pitched so low that it rumbled over her skin. "Once you're mine, it's forever."

With a boldness that stunned them both, Olympia met his gaze and uttered the words that would alter everything in their relationship. "Then make me yours. Because it's all I can think about and I don't ever want to be anyone else's."

GRIFFIN STARED down at her upturned face and allowed the reality of the moment to sink in, to fully grasp the fact that he wasn't simply entertaining an elaborate fantasy. When she didn't draw away from him or shrink back, he clasped his arms about her and tugged her against him. Feeling the weight of her crushed against him, he reveled in it.

It was a dream, surely. Nothing so perfect had occurred in his life in such a long time that he feared it wasn't real. Was it madness? Had it finally taken him and this sweet vision before him was just a cruel twist of his own mind? Ultimately, it was of no matter. She felt real in his arms, and when he bent his head to take her lips, they tasted sweet beneath his own. If it wasn't reality, but some mad and fevered fantasy, he no longer cared.

He kissed her intently, desperately—plying her lips with his. Each contour and curve was mapped beneath his lips, tested by his tongue. He nipped at her lips and felt her shiver in his arms. It was glorious.

He rose, pulling her up with him, his lips never leaving hers. Testing their pillowy softness between his teeth, he nipped at them slightly less than gently. A part of him was appalled, reminding himself that she was a virgin and completely untutored in such things. But she didn't appear frightened.

A soft sigh escaped her parted lips and he could feel the hardened peaks of her breasts pressed against him through the layers of her clothing. He wanted to strip away every one of them, to reveal the lush curves and soft skin beneath.

With that thought, that temptation, spurring his actions, he reached for the laces of her gown and began to tug them free. When the fabric had loosened enough, he pushed it down her arms, to her waist, baring the chemise and stays beneath. If he'd been capable of thought, he might have taken note of how worn her garments were, but his sole preoccupation was with what lay beneath. The mounds of her breasts were pushed up by her stays and he wanted nothing more than to taste that tender flesh.

Lacing the fingers of one hand into the simple bun that she always seemed to wear, he titled her head back. Her neck arched gracefully and it was as necessary to him as breathing to kiss her there, to trace that pale column with his tongue and tease it with the sharp sting of his teeth. Her soft gasp ended on a sharper moan as he bent her back further and pressed a kiss between her breasts. A shiver followed and he smiled against her skin.

Griffin realized that he would never have to wonder with Olympia. Every thing she felt was written clearly upon her face, and very little of what was going on in her mind was hidden from him. She had her secrets, she'd said, but he couldn't imagine anything in her past as dark as what he'd shared. Even if it were so, he couldn't imagine that it would alter his feelings for her at all.

It was that which gave him pause. He did have feelings

for Olympia. A strange mix of desire and protectiveness, but also an eager curiosity about her, to know what was in her mind, what her thoughts and opinions were. It would be easier if it were simply lust but even the fear sparked by the realization that his emotions were far more engaged than he wanted them to be was not enough to make him back away from her. There was no power on earth or possibly beyond that would make him give her up at that moment.

Unable to resist the lure of the plump mounds of her breasts for a moment longer, he tugged at her stays. The fabric shifted, freeing first one lush, rounded globe and then the other. The perfection of her pale, milky skin was only rivaled by the sweet temptation of her pert, rose colored nipples. So he didn't resist. He allowed his lips to coast over her skin, down, trailing hot kisses that left her shuddering in his arms. But when his mouth closed over one taut peak, she let out a sharp cry and clutched at him desperately.

Savoring the taste of her skin, the velvety feel of it beneath his tongue, he wanted to drive her wild—to feel her coming apart for him. Griffin lifted her into his arms and crossed the room quickly. Laying her back on the bed, he tugged at her gown and her petticoat until they slipped over her hips. Her boots came next, tossed aside with her gown. Only then did he pause to drink in the sight of her.

Pale, creamy skin barely covered beneath the threadbare muslin of her chemise and her worn stays. He circled her ankle with one hand, lifting her foot to his chest, he trailed his hands along her calf, her knee and then over the silken skin of her thigh. As he reached her garter, he untied it and then rolled the stocking down her leg. He repeated the process until her legs were completely bared.

"I had intended a slow seduction... to set all your doubts and fears to rest first," he said, even as he skimmed her chemise higher on her hips.

She didn't reply immediately, just watched him, her gaze tracking the movements of his hands on her thighs. Their gazes met and then she simply reached up and tugged at the laces of her stays. It loosened, then parted entirely. He helped her to remove it completely and then her chemise as well.

His breath hitched in his lungs and his whole body burned with need—to claim, to conquer, to possess her entirely. Griffin moved over her, resting his weight on his elbows as he cupped her breasts in his hands. He moved his thumbs over the crests, teasing them until she cried out. She was restless beneath him, seeking an unknown relief.

One hand slid from her breast, over her ribs and down to the soft mound of her stomach. He moved lower and she instinctively clenched her thighs together.

Griffin kissed her again, his lips coasting from her lips, along her jaw line to the soft shell of her ear. He whispered, "Let me in, Olympia. Open for me, sweet."

∾

OLYMPIA COULDN'T BREATHE. Her whole body felt as if it were on fire. Deep within her, it raged, and every touch stoked it to new heights. It should have been shocking, to lie there naked in his embrace but she reveled in it. And at his whispered command, she fought against every instinct and parted her thighs for him.

As his hand delved between them, his fingers parted her slick flesh and stroked her in such a way that she could do nothing but cry out and cling to him. It robbed her of sense, of any reason and it sparked a new kind of desperation inside her. The need was insistent, driving, all consuming.

"Griffin, I can't think. I don't know what to do!"

He smiled against her skin, pressed soft kisses to her neck, her collar bone, as his fingers moved over her with a skill that melted everything inside her. "You don't have to do anything, Olympia. And you don't have to think... you only have to feel."

So she did. She gave herself up to the sensations he sparked inside her, her hips arching upward to meet his questing fingers. Tension coiled deep within her, building to something she didn't understand but that she still strained toward. Reaching out, she clutched at him, her nails digging into his flesh as her body bowed beneath his.

It happened suddenly, every muscle drawing taut, her thighs quivering. Her whole body trembled as the release washed through her. Lights danced behind her eyes as she shuddered in his arms, his name falling from her lips on a desperate cry.

"That's it, my sweet," he murmured. "Let it take you."

She had no choice in the matter. It was as if her mind and body were no longer connected, overwhelmed by the passion he'd stirred in her and the completion he'd brought her to. When he moved between her thighs completely, bringing her legs up to wrap around him, Olympia was almost ashamed of her eagerness. But she wanted to know what else would occur, and she desperately wanted to give him the same pleasure he'd brought her.

The sensation of him pressing into her, filling her was so very different from the tender stroking of his fingers. This was more primal, and while it wasn't exactly pleasurable, she still felt compelled to urge him on, to take what he offered her greedily.

He moved deeper and she felt a tearing sensation followed by a burning pain. It dissipated quickly and only the strange sensation of fullness remained. When he thrust his hips again, driving deeper, Olympia felt that same burning need building again. But it was more insistent, more urgent. Every thrust drove her closer to that now familiar edge. Hitching her thighs higher on his firm hips, she savored each stroke and the climb. Her belly drew taut and quivered against him. Her thighs trembled as she rocked her hips against him, accepting each surge of him within her with an eagerness that should have shamed her. Her hands roamed his back, sliding lower to cup his firm buttocks as he drove into her again.

She shattered. The world fractured around her and nothing existed but the points of contact between their bodies. As she clenched around him, her muscles spasming with her release, he thrust again and then uttered her name on a harsh growl. Abruptly, he withdrew from her and she felt something warm and wet on her thigh.

Griffin slumped against her, pressing his forehead to her shoulder as his ragged breath fanned over her skin. Olympia closed her arms about him, holding him close. It wasn't romance. It certainly wasn't love. It was something darker, deeper... even animalistic. And it made her feel alive in ways she'd never known existed.

CHAPTER SIXTEEN

OLYMPIA AWOKE SLOWLY AND STRETCHED. Her body ached, subtle reminders of all that she'd done with Griffin the night before. Recalling all that had transpired between them the day before, and again during the night, she could feel a heated blush creeping up her neck as Collins bustled into the room carrying a breakfast tray.

After a jaw cracking yawn, Olympia sat up in bed, clutching the covers to her chest to hide the fact that she wore nothing beneath the bedclothes. She'd donned a nightrail at some point, but Griffin had quickly disposed of it. The decadence of sleeping naked in his arms had been an eye opening experience for her. She'd realized that intimacy went far beyond just the act of lovemaking.

"You've slept very late, m'lady!" Collins said as she

bustled about the room. "And that hair looks like a bird nested in it!"

"Collins," Olympia said reprovingly.

The maid blushed, realizing she'd said something inappropriate. "My apologies, m'lady. I do forget myself at times. Tis an odd business being a lady's maid!"

"I'm sure it is," Olympia agreed. "Would you fetch my wrapper?"

Collins looked at her sharply. It wasn't typical for Olympia to have her fetch and carry so much, but as she was completely nude beneath the covers, she could hardly cross the room and get it herself.

The maid returned to her side with it and gave her a questioning look. "We won't be returning to London, will we, m'lady?"

Olympia blushed. "No, Collins, we will not. For better or worse, we are remaining here. Neither Lady Florence nor Mrs. Webster will be able to refute my right to be here now."

Collins shuddered delicately. "They won't like it, m'lady. Not at all. I think it'll only make them more dangerous."

The maid was more than likely correct. "We'll be cautious. Both of us."

"Yes, m'lady... and I'd avoid her today at all costs, if possible. Seems one of the newer footmen spurned her advances last night and she's in rare form. Broke everything in her chamber she could lift to throw."

Which meant she'd be out for blood, and she already had

a taste for Olympia's. "Thank you, Collins... I'll try to avoid her."

"Won't be possible, my lady," Collins said smartly as she laid out the new gown she'd been working tirelessly to complete. "Not in this house. I've a word of advice, and you can take it or you can sack me for it... That woman is not to be trusted. I'd have her out of this house as soon as I could if I were you. And to be even bolder, if you mean to press his lordship to do what you ask, now would be the time. Also, Mrs. Webster has asked to see you."

Olympia grimaced at that. "Tell her I'm indisposed."

Collins shook her head vigorously. "No, m'lady. I'll not do it. You show her any hint of weakness and she'll chew you up and spit you out.

Her maid was right. Any hint of cowardice would only make things more difficult later on. She had to face her, whether she wanted to or not.

Olympia nodded and lifted the cover from her breakfast tray. The aroma of fresh kippers and eggs had her mouth watering. "Fine. Have a bath prepared for me, Collins, while I enjoy my breakfast."

"Yes, m'lady. I imagine you've quite the appetite this morning," the young woman offered with a cheeky grin as she left the room.

After Collins left, and Olympia's blush had faded to a reasonable degree, she made short work of the food. Climbing from the bed, she donned her wrapper and crossed the room to the connecting door between her chamber and Griffin's. She knocked softly, and he called out for her to enter.

Olympia stepped through the door and paused. He was naked, fresh from the bath. Water still glistened on his dark skin. Her gaze focused on one lone droplet that hovered at the base of his throat and then slid down, winding over his chest in a way that made her want to press her lips to his skin and trace each droplet with her tongue.

Even as she thought it, her eyes traveled lower. His body hardened beneath her gaze, his shaft growing thicker and longer. "I had wanted to speak to you about Lady Florence," she finally managed to choke out.

"Well, that would effectively wither any man," he said sharply.

Olympia's gaze remained fixed on his member. "It seems to have no effect on you."

"It's counteracted completely by your alluring presence," he replied. "But I imagine that you are not here to aid me with my morning affliction."

"No," she said, though her tone was less than certain. "Collins informed me that she's in high dudgeon. Rejected by a footman and having a tantrum, to put it bluntly. I think we should send her to the dower house. I do not trust her, Griffin, and I fear she means to do you irreparable harm."

He sighed wearily and dropped the towel he'd been using as he reached for his small clothes. "Olympia, I will gladly send her to the dower house once it is habitable, but you must stop seeing plots and machinations where none exist. No, Florence is not to be trusted, but do not give her more credit than she deserves. The woman is obsessed with clothes and handsome footmen. As long as those needs are met, she'll be no trouble at all."

"If I give her too much credit, you give her too little... That woman is a viper and if you do not see it, you've willfully blinded yourself."

He pulled his breeches on, his movements agitated and clearly annoyed with the topic. "I cannot toss her out without her having a place to go and, at this time, the dower house is not an option. The roof is leaking and the place hasn't been cleaned in more than a year!"

As she looked at him, Olympia realized that he was utterly exhausted. He'd spent the evening making love to her, and had continued well into the night. She'd woken up in the wee hours of the morning to the sounds of awful screams filtering down the hallway. She'd seen him slipping out of her chamber to attend his sister.

His present mood had nothing to do with their current disagreement. It wasn't Florence. It wasn't even her. It wasn't even that he was beyond physically and mentally exhausted. It was frustration, because he was running out of options and time. The new medication he'd prepared for her had worked for some time, but was already losing its potency. The wailing and screaming had grown in intensity throughout the night until dawn when it had abruptly halted. All of those things had mixed and mingled to form his current dark mood, and she wasn't helping him. At the moment she was only adding to his already overwhelming problems.

"I didn't say it had to be immediate! But we both know that there will be no peace in this house while she is here!"

"Fine," he agreed. "I will send workman to the dower house to begin repairs as soon as the roads have cleared and I will inform Florence that we mean to send her there. But if you expect that to bring us any peace at all, you are sadly mistaken."

In the course of their conversation, he'd dressed entirely, save for his neckcloth which most of the time he eschewed anyway. He struggled into his boots and then left without a backward glance.

Turning on her heel, Olympia retreated to her own room. She'd won the battle but there had been a cost.

"That could have gone better," Collins said. She'd apparently returned during their discussion and overheard everything. Olympia gave her a baleful stare as the maid added rose scented oil to the freshly drawn bath. Two other maids entered, each one baring a bucket of steaming water which was added to the tub. When they left and only Collins remained, Olympia removed her wrapper and climbed into the tub.

It was pointless to correct Collins' behavior or to try and treat her as simply a maid. They were conspirators, in plain point of fact. Between them, they shared the dark and ugly secret that had prompted Olympia's hasty withdrawal from London, her reason for willingly accepting marriage sight unseen to a man she'd never even heard of. They were, in all likelihood, murderers as there was little possibility that her uncle would have survived, much less completely recover from the blows to the head that the two of them had delivered. She was quickly learning that the best way to deal with much of Collins' inappropriate behavior was to simply refrain from acknowledging it at all.

Olympia sank deeper into the heated water and bit back a sigh of relief. Keeping Florence and her machinations out of their lives was the most important thing. And Mrs. Webster would have to follow, she decided. Whatever it took, that woman was another viper and her strange hold over the house needed to be abolished.

When her bath was completed, Olympia sat on the small ottoman before the fire as Collins combed out her hair. The heat from the fire, would help it to dry quicker.

"I've no hand for the curling tongs, m'lady, but mayhap if we braid your hair and let it dry we can get a nice wave to it."

"That would be fine, Collins. Thank you."

When the task was complete, her damp hair arranged in a series of braids and then pinned up in a simple coronet, she dressed in the new gown that Collins had created for her. The green wool fit her to perfection, though the neckline was a bit deeper than she was typically comfortable with.

"Perhaps a fichu?"

"No," Collins said. "You want his lordship to be in a better mood, don't you?"

"Yes," Olympia replied.

"Then showing a bit of bosom is a good way to start," the maid said of matter-of-factly.

Curiosity warred with common sense and Olympia felt compelled to ask. "Tell me the truth about your past employers, Collins, before you came to my aunt and uncle. I know you were never a lady's maid and if memory serves me correctly, you were not a very good scullery maid, either."

The woman's thin face scrunched as she considered her options. "Very well, m'lady. My mother worked as a wardrobe mistress for a theater... but not a fancy sort of theater where respectable folk would go. It was... well most would call it indecent. And rightly so, I reckon."

"How indecent?" Olympia asked.

"Most of the women what worked there were more light skirt than dancer or actress," the maid admitted.

"And you made clothes for them... Costumes?"

Collins raised an eyebrow. "Yes, m'lady. Well, helped my mother with them. As she got older, her hands stiffened up and her eyes weren't what they used to be. Helping her turned into just doing the work m'self. Though the gowns I made were hardly anything that would be fitting for you. "

"I don't mean to wear it to dinner, Collins," she said, thoughtfully. "But... I imagine you could fashion me something suitable to wear for my husband in the privacy of our chamber?"

The maid smiled. "Aye, m'lady. I can. His eyes will fair pop out and I daresay you'll get anything you ask for."

A peaceful home with him, free from the influence of people who intended to harm either of them. That was all she wanted. To feel *safe* again, she realized. It was something she hadn't experienced since before her parents' deaths. Griffin hadn't either, she was certain, though the difficulties they had faced were very different.

With her morning toilette completed, Olympia braced herself for the coming confrontation with Mrs. Webster. Leaving her room, she took a deep breath and straightened her spine. She found the housekeeper in the hall just at top of the stairs.

"I see you've finally decided to leave your bed. And his," the housekeeper said disapprovingly.

"You overstep, Mrs. Webster," Olympia snapped. "What occurs between my husband and myself in the privacy of our chambers is none of your concern."

Mrs. Webster smiled coolly. "You may think that you've won... that by seducing him you've gained the upper hand, but rest assured, m'lady, the things I know about this family he will never want made public."

Cold fury washed through her. "Do not threaten me, Mrs. Webster. And do not threaten my husband. You are in his employ but that can change at any time!"

Mrs. Webster's smile faded into a gruesome snarl. "Mr. Swindon might have had the final choice in bride for his lordship, but I made certain that he gathered enough information about you to keep you well in hand! I know about your uncle! I know why your aunt was so eager to have you married off and out of her home!"

Cold dread washed through her. She hadn't told Griffin about her uncle's advances, about the lengths she'd had to go to in order to avoid being ruined by him. The shame of it was something she'd hoped never to share with anyone. She hadn't told Mr. Swindon about the final night, the night when her desperate attempts to save her virtue had resulted in grave injury to him. Had it not been for Collins, her uncle would have raped and murdered her that night. Mrs. Webster couldn't possibly know everything, but she possessed enough information to get to the truth if she chose.

"I have nothing to hide, Mrs. Webster. You will not rule in this house forever," Olympia brazened. She would be certain of it. "And if you think to use his sister against him—."

The woman grabbed her arm, twisting it painfully as she dragged her toward one of the unoccupied chambers. "What do you know of Cassandra?" Mrs. Webster demanded.

Olympia yanked her wrist free of the other woman's grasp. "He took me to her room last night. I know about her condition and I know that you've helped him to care for her! But that doesn't excuse what you've done here, and if you ever manhandle me in such a way again, I will be certain that you regret it!"

"You know nothing," the woman sneered at her. "You don't know the hell I've endured in this house... that my mother and grandmother endured in this house as we nursed one member of this family after another through madness! We've covered up their atrocities, we've lied for them, protected them, and yet he brought you here! This is *my house*. It will *always* be my house!"

"Oh, la! What a party I've missed!"

Olympia would have groaned at the sound of Lady Florence's voice but she wouldn't take her eyes off Mrs. Webster. Any distraction from the woman in front of her could prove disastrous. Griffin feared he was going mad, but in surveying Mrs. Webster, Olympia realized he was not the one who should fear it. The housekeeper was nigh to insane herself, paranoid and dangerous.

"I'm returning to my room, Mrs. Webster. Do not summon me again. And I will be speaking to my husband about this," Olympia warned softly and then backed away from her before she cleared the door and fled.

FLORENCE LOUNGED against the drawing room door and smirked at the dour housekeeper. "You've overplayed your hand, Mrs. Webster. You should have allowed me to guide you in this."

"And what would you have done?" the housekeeper demanded.

"You have access to the perfect weapon, Mrs. Webster," Florence offered mildly. "Someone who could easily rid us both of our troublesome new viscountess... Griffin would be consumed with guilt and therefore easily led. All you have to do... is leave the door unlocked."

"She might hurt someone else," the housekeeper protested.

"She might," Florence agreed. "But it won't be us. We'll be safely behind locked doors. Whether it's a housemaid, a footman, or his lovely new viscountess, he will still blame himself. And he will blame her... because she's distracted him from his true purpose of curing his sister. We win, either way."

"And if Cassandra is hurt?"

Florence's eyes widened. "You do truly care for her, don't you?"

"She was a sweet child, until she came here. Until your husband got his hands on her!"

"We were all sweet children until that happened," Florence replied bitterly. "Do it, Mrs. Webster. It's the only way."

The housekeeper wavered for a moment, before squaring her shoulders. "No. Not yet. I will consider it, and if things become dire, then I shall. But when I mentioned her family in London, she was nervous. Scared even."

Florence considered that. "Fine. I'll start there and see what else I can find... Get one of the maids to cozy up to that stick like harridan she has with her. The least likely lady's maid I've ever encountered!"

Mrs. Webster nodded her assent. "Yes, my lady. I will let you know what I find. I don't wish to jeopardize Cassandra anymore than necessary. She's far more fragile than you realize."

"We cannot afford to take too much time, Mrs. Webster. The longer she has with him, the more likely he is to fall under her sway. Never underestimate the power a wife holds over a husband... Griffin is a romantic at heart. He will fall in love with her because that is simply his nature. And when that happens, neither of us will hold any power in this house."

Florence exited the room with a swish of her skirts. The housekeeper would consider it, but eventually, she would relent. It was only a matter of time.

CHAPTER SEVENTEEN

A HEADACHE HAD BEEN Olympia's convenient excuse to avoid the dining room that evening. It wasn't the room's bloody history that bothered her. She simply wished to avoid another skirmish with either Mrs. Webster or Lady Florence.

Seated at her dressing table, she waited patiently as Collins as slowly and meticulous removed each pin from her hair. They really would have to do something about her lack of knowledge as a hairdresser.

The connecting door opened and Griffin stood there. He'd dressed for dinner but upon his return had discarded his cravat and coat. His waistcoat was undone and his shirt was open at the neck. He looked disreputable, even a bit rakish, and far more appealing than he should for her peace of mind.

"You may leave us, Collins," he said. "If her ladyship requires any further assistance, I will provide it."

The maid blushed, bobbed a curtsy, and fled the room as if being chased by a hellhound. In the mirror, Olympia gave him a baleful glance as the door slammed behind the departing figure of her maid. "You terrify her!"

"Do I terrify you?" he asked.

"Hardly," she replied.

"Even when I'm in a ghastly, foul mood and take it out on you?" The question was posed as he stepped deeper into the room. He held a piece of cloth in his hand, tied up to form a pouch.

"What do you have there?" she asked curiously.

He placed it on the dressing table before her. "A bribe... I'm hoping to buy my way back into your good graces."

Olympia untied the knotted ends of what appeared to be a napkin. When it fell open, her mouth watered instantly. Claiming illness had offered Mrs. Webster the perfect revenge. She'd sent up a tray bearing thin, greasy gruel and stale bread for her dinner, claiming that it was what she needed to recover from her illness. Griffin had purloined slices of ham and cheese, as well as fresh, crusty bread. There was even a sliced apple.

"You were never *out* of my good graces," she replied evenly. "Though if you were, this is precisely how to get back into them."

Olympia was too busy eating to see his answering smile. If she had looked at him, she would have noted that he stared at her not just with passion but with a tenderness that would have surprised them both.

"I was in a foul mood this morning," he offered. "I wished to apologize for the manner in which I spoke to you. It was wrong. You did not deserve it and I will endeavor to do better in the future."

She glanced up again, her mouth full of the delicious and forbidden treats he'd brought. When she finally managed to swallow, she said, "I knew you'd been up all hours of the night. It was the wrong time to press you about such matters."

He settled onto the edge of her bed. "I want you to understand, Olympia that I would send them both away if I could... Mrs. Webster and Lady Florence. I know they are thick as thieves and hatching plots. But they both have access to information about me, about this family, and about the house that could ruin us forever. And if we are ruined, it will have far reaching consequences."

"I don't understand."

Griffin paused, and then bent to remove his boots. It was a clear indication that he meant to stay and a new hunger replaced Olympia's desire for food altogether.

"My uncle invested poorly for the most part and lost several fortunes. There were a few successful investments that are still producing... a shipping company in Liverpool, there is a salt mine to the south that is still doing well. And I've poured yet more funds into those businesses and people know it. If the family secrets that Mrs. Webster and Florence are privy to come out, no one will deal with those businesses... they will fail because the Darkes have been associated with them. And that's nothing compared to the tenant farmers. What will become of them when local merchants refuse to do business with them? They'll have no place to sell their eggs, meat, or wool; they'll have no place to buy the supplies they need to survive."

Those words quelled her burgeoning desire. "They would destroy everyone just to destroy you. I know that. Neither of them possesses the ability to see beyond their own selfish agendas to even consider the consequences of their actions to others."

"Precisely. So, I will keep Mrs. Webster mollified. I will watch Florence like a hawk and attempt to rein her in when necessary. But we must try to appease them... whether we like it or not. At least for now."

Olympia returned the uneaten food to the napkin he'd used to spirit it to her. After tying it up, she rose and walked toward him.

"I will try to remember that there is a valid reason for holding my tongue... but they do try me greatly," she offered.

He reached out, latching his hands onto her hips and tugging her forward until he could fold her in his arms completely. His head was pressed to her, just beneath her bosom and his hands roamed freely over her calves and thighs as he tugged her nightrail upward.

"Let us not think of them anymore tonight," he urged.

"We are newly wed, after all. It is a time to be obsessively devoted to one another—to the exclusion of all else."

Olympia sighed as his hands roamed the backs of her thighs, squeezing and caressing with deliberate intent. "You could tempt a saint."

"I've no wish to tempt a saint," he offered, lifting his head and pressing a hot kiss to her breast through the fabric of her nightrail and wrapper. "I only wish to tempt my wife. Have I?"

"You know you have!"

"Prove it me," he said. "Let me see you. All of you."

"You saw me yesterday afternoon... and last night," she protested, embarrassed.

"Mere glimpses, Olympia. And I was lost in such a state of lust that I fear I did not pay proper homage to all of your charms... Take off your wrapper," he asked, giving a playful tug to the ties that held it closed.

Olympia's face burned at the thought. He had seen her, but it all seemed different now. To disrobe completely while he remained fully clothed seemed especially wicked somehow. Yet, she was reaching for the ties, loosening them and letting the garment fall even as her doubts shouted and clamored within her mind. It appeared he could talk her into anything.

When her wrapper lay discarded on the floor, and only the thin fabric of her nightrail covered her body, he pushed her away from him just a bit. His gaze traveled over her hungrily, so intently that she felt it almost like a caress.

"The rest of it, Olympia," he said. "I want all of you bared to me... to look at you at my leisure and savor the perfection of your body."

"I am far from perfect," she protested, embarrassed at such overblown praise.

"You are," he insisted. "Porcelain skin so soft I can scarce believe it is real, breasts that beg for my touch, to be taken in my mouth... Shall I go on? You blush so prettily when I've scandalized you thoroughly."

"Will you stop saying such things if I remove my nightrail?" she asked.

"If you remove that garment, Olympia, I can assure you that neither of us will be saying very much at all for some time to come," he promised.

Her mouth went dry and her heart raced in her chest. It was a challenge, but the reward he offered was beyond her ability to resist. With trembling fingers, she reached up and loosened the ties of her nightrail, drawing it open until it simply fell from her shoulders and pooled on the floor. Standing in front of him, she felt vulnerable in ways she'd never imagined. But as she saw his eyes darken, his gaze traveling over her body— that sense of vulnerability faded. Instead, she began to feel powerful. His hunger for her was evident in his expression, in the rapidness of his breathing and the heavy weight of his gaze upon her.

"You almost make me believe I am beautiful when you look at me that way," she said with wonder.

"Come closer," he urged. "I will convince you yet."

Olympia did as he asked, moving closer to him, but he when she was standing between his parted knees, he didn't tug her onto the bed with him as she'd expected. Instead, he held her there, his hands moving over her, mapping every curve and contour of her body even as his mouth followed. His lips burned a trail along her rib cage, the underside of her breast. When he bit her there, his teeth grazing the tender flesh, she let out a soft yelp of surprise. But what shocked her even more was that she'd enjoyed it thoroughly.

"You are wicked," she muttered.

"As are you," he replied softly, his breath fanning over one furled nipple. "Do you deny that everything I've done to you and with you, that every touch, has brought you pleasure?"

"No. It would be a lie." Her response was breathless, her voice thin and weak as he was tracing delicate circles on the crest of her hip bone, each one inching closer to the juncture of her thighs where she was already wet for him.

He drew her down then, slipping his knees between her thighs and parting them until she sat astride him. They were face to face, her breasts pressed against the hard wall of his chest. Even through his breeches she could feel the hard press of his arousal against her. It was an instinctive thing to move against him, to rock her hips against his hardness. It eased the ache growing inside her for just a moment, but when it returned, its force was even greater.

He reached between them, unbuttoning the fall of his breeches. Olympia leaned back glanced down, embarrassed but also eager to see him. She'd been too shy to look at him the night before.

Curiosity got the better of her, and with tentative fingers, she stroked the domed crown. His breath hissed out between clenched teeth and she stopped immediately.

"Don't," he said. "It feels wonderful when you touch me that way."

Olympia did as he bade, exploring the hard length of him, learning the satiny texture of his skin, the impossible firmness of his flesh. Knowing that she pleased him, that it only intensified his desire for her spurred her own desire to new heights. The ache at her center, the sharp and nagging need that only he could fulfill, grew beyond her ability to bear.

As if he'd read her mind and new precisely what she needed from him, he cupped his hand around hers, and with it, guided his rigid length to her entrance. It was an instinctive thing, to simply allow her hips to sink lower, taking him inside her.

The sensation of fullness was still novel to her, and the pleasure it brought still a marvel. His hands fell to her hips, lifting her and then bringing her down again. Olympia bit her lip, trying in vain to hold back the pleasured moan.

"Don't," he urged, stroking his thumb over her lip. "Let me hear you. Don't hide anything from me."

He surged into her again, and any thoughts of embarrassment, any thought at all, faded. Clinging to him, Olympia dug her nails into the heavy muscles of his shoulders, letting her head fall back as a soft cry escaped her.

Every movement brought a wealth of new sensations, every thrust of his body into hers took the blinding pleasure to new heights. She could feel it building within her, the tension coiling tighter. Every muscle drew taut as she hovered on that precipice.

Griffin leaned forward, kissed her neck and then bit her there. His teeth scraped over her tender skin as he pressed deep one last time. Olympia simply came apart. There was no other word for it. Her body was wracked with tremors as waves of pleasure washed through her. She clung to him desperately. He stood then, bore her back onto the bed and thrust once, and again, before withdrawing from her completely. The warmth of his release bathed her thigh.

Precautions, he'd said. The term made infinitely more sense to her now. The perfection of the moment faded for her. But she'd agreed to his terms and she'd abide by it. To do otherwise would be dishonorable.

He sank onto the bed beside her, pulling her into his arms. She went willingly, grateful for the warmth and comfort of his embrace. Children hadn't really been something she'd allowed herself to dream of for the last several years because the possibility of marriage had seemed so impossibly far away. And now, with a husband who desired her, even if love was not to be part of their arrangement— that yearning was growing within her. She resented it, but part of her also resented him. It was unfair and she knew it. He'd been honest with her from the start about that. She would have to make her peace with it, one way or another.

CHAPTER EIGHTEEN

My Lord Darke,

Please forgive me for being absent so long from Darkwood Hall. I am sure you are quite curious as to why it has taken so long for me to complete the business matters in London as you requested. In short, my lord, I am a coward and am avoiding facing certain dismissal as a result of disobeying your orders.

My only defense, my lord, is that I have worked for your family for many years. Before your mother passed away, she requested that I look after you. In disobeying your orders, I am fulfilling my promise to her. Rather than procuring the bride you requested, I attempted to procure the bride that I felt would suit you best.

If I have succeeded in doing so, I will happily await your

instruction as to any further business inquiries I should make for you in London. If I have not succeeded, then this letter will serve as my resignation.

My apologies if I have overstepped, my lord. But in all fairness, I must state that Lady Darke, formerly Miss Olympia Daventry, appears very much to be a damsel in distress and though she would hardly appreciate the description, I do hope that you will provide whatever assistance she may need should you deem to terminate the union I have forced upon you.

YOUR HUMBLE AND LOYAL, *but far from obedient servant,*
    Hon. Jasper Swindon, Esquire

GRIFFIN READ THE LETTER AGAIN. Mr. Swindon's apologies for disobeying a direct order were quite eloquent. They had also come late enough that the wily old fox knew full well that annulment would no longer be an option.

Still, try as he might, Griffin could not be angry at him. He should be, by all rights, but it would be disingenuous. Any anger he might once have had was overwhelmed by gratitude and by the relief of knowing that Olympia was his.

Sitting at his desk, Griffin penned a brief list of instructions regarding investments he wished to have made on his behalf. He also gave specific instructions as to a gift he wished to obtain for Olympia. If that didn't allay the old man's fears of having chosen poorly, nothing would, Griffin thought.

With that done, he rose and headed toward the breakfast room. Olympia would be up and he found that he was eager for the sight of her, but that was not a new occurrence.

ENTERING THE BREAKFAST ROOM, Olympia paused just inside the door. Griffin was there, but so was Lady Florence. They appeared to have been in quite a heated exchange when she entered, if the broken crockery and wide-eyed footmen were any indication. The tension in the air was palpable.

"I would wish you a good morning," Griffin said softly, "But I fear it isn't a possibility anymore."

"I should go. I'll have a tray sent up," she offered.

"Don't rush off, darling girl!" Lady Florence cooed. Her voice was deceptively sweet but there was murder in her eyes. "We've ever so much to talk about. Dear Griffin was just telling me that I'm to be banished. Strange that I should be tossed from my home only after you've arrived to occupy it!"

"Enough," Griffin said. Though he spoke softly, there was a wealth of warning infused into that single word.

"Fine," Lady Florence relented. "I'll behave. You may enjoy your breakfast in relative peace and quiet!"

When she made no move to leave, Olympia asked, "Are you remaining here then?"

"I did say relative peace and quiet," Lady Florence replied snarkily. "Is my presence so disturbing to you that you cannot even bear it when I sit quietly in the same room?"

"Not at all," Olympia replied as she moved to the sideboard and began to fill her plate. "I simply wasn't aware that you were capable of sitting quietly."

Griffin coughed softly, camouflaging a laugh. Taking a seat at the table to his right, Olympia offered him a conspiratorial smile.

"You received a letter yesterday," he said. "I meant to tell you last night but I forgot."

"Who is it from? Mr. Swindon?"

"No," Griffin replied, retrieving the envelope from the pocket of his waistcoat. "It was enclosed with correspondence from Mr. Swindon to me. Apparently, your aunt sought him out and asked him to see that you received it."

Olympia felt the blood rain from her face. She clutched the edge of the table and willed herself not to faint. "I see," she finally managed and took the letter from his outstretched hand. Ignoring his look of concern, she tucked it into the pocket of her morning gown.

"Well, don't keep us in suspense, darling!" Lady Florence cooed. "Tell us what news you've had from home!"

Turning to Griffin, Lady Florence continued in a smug tone, "You know, Lady Darke and I were having the most interesting conversation yesterday! I asked her what sort of life she'd been living in London that would make her amenable to the idea of marrying a complete stranger and traveling off to some isolated house in the middle of nowhere. I suppose it's true what they say... speak of the devil, and he shall appear... or in this case just send a note."

"Are you all right?" he asked her softly.

"I'm quite fine. Just concerned that it might be a bit of bad news. My uncle had taken ill before I left," she offered the too pat explanation and hoped that both Griffin and Lady Florence would accept it.

"Then open your letter, dear, and let us all know the poor man's fate!"

Olympia glared across the table at Lady Florence, annoyed by her insistence and the sing-song tone she seemed to prefer when goading her. With hands that trembled, she opened the letter and scanned the first paragraph. Cold dread washed through her.

It was even worse than she'd expected. Her uncle hadn't died, after all. Rather, he'd made a miraculous recovery. While he couldn't yet speak clearly, her aunt stated, he was struggling to regain full function and would undoubtedly be able to tell them everything that had happened the night of his accident.

There was no mistaking the tone of the letter. Her aunt knew something. She suspected that Olympia must have had something to do with her husband's accident. With her palms sweating and her heart racing, Olympia replaced the letter in her pocket. Collins would have to be told.

"It appears my uncle has made a miraculous recovery... I fear I'm quite overwhelmed by the news. If you'll excuse me," she said and rose on knees that trembled.

GRIFFIN WATCHED with growing concern as Olympia fled the small dining room. Whatever had been in that letter had upset her terribly.

"Secrets are such ugly things," Florence said, her voice grating on him.

"Don't you have a footman to bed?" he asked pointedly.

"I've worn him out, I'm afraid," she said with a smile. "He's lovely, but he lacks stamina."

Griffin closed his eyes, disgusted by her and by the forced cohabitation. "Calling you a lady is an insult to the rest of them," he said, and rose from the table.

"And is your lovely bride a lady?" she asked, her voice sharp enough to cut like glass. "Or is she a wildcat in your bed? So demure and yet she cries out so lustily for you in the night... I daresay her screams might even drown out Cassandra's! But then you always were impressive. You look every inch the gentleman but fuck like a field hand."

"You're leaving this house," he said. "Today. I won't have you tormenting us any further!"

"I can't. I've nowhere to go," she said. "Alas, Lady Jane Darlington was my only remaining friend in Liverpool and she's gotten herself into a bit of a pickle. Her husband has taken her off to the wilds of Scotland and hired a house filled with only female servants and ugly old men. Poor dear. Such a sad fate."

"Then I'll be sending for workman to begin repairs on the dower house immediately... even if it is the dead of winter. I can't abide your presence here a moment longer."

Lady Florence sipped her tea, her manners perfect and her face a mien of loveliness. "I do wonder what was in that letter," she said, as she lowered her cup. "She didn't look to be overwhelmed with relief or joy at the notion that her uncle had recovered... I would actually say that her expression appeared to be one of sheer terror. Why do you think that is?"

He meant to find out, Griffin thought. And whatever it was, he meant to be certain that information never fell into Florence's hands. "Do not think to press her, to question her, or to vex her in anyway. I've allowed you free rein in this house, you and that termagant, Mrs. Webster. But I won't see her harmed by either of you. If that means tossing you both out and damn the consequences, then so be it. Tread carefully, Florence."

In her chamber, Olympia waited for Collins. She'd rung for the girl only moments earlier but it felt like ages. As she read through the letter again, she wondered if it truly was a veiled threat or if she were simply as paranoid as Mrs. Webster.

When Collins finally entered, Olympia couldn't even speak. Instead, she just thrust the letter at the maid. Collins dutifully took it. As she read the words, her hands began to tremble.

"Do you think she knows, m'lady?" the younger woman asked, her voice a terrified whisper.

"I think she suspects. She can't *know* for certain, but if he regains his ability to speak, she certainly will. We both know he'll tell. And it won't be the true version of events, either! It'll be us plotting against him instead of—." Olympia broke off, unable to say aloud what he'd meant to do, what he'd try to do half a dozen times before that night.

In the year and a half since her parents' deaths, she'd narrowly avoided ruin at his hands on more occasions than she cared to admit. It was always worse when he'd been drinking. He'd groped her, tried to kiss her, but when he was drinking, there was a meanness in him that wouldn't be stopped.

She'd made it a point to never be alone, but that night, she'd been careless. No, she corrected, not careless—just exhausted. Her aunt had set her to beating the rugs until her neck and shoulders had ached horribly. She'd gone to the kitchen to fetch the liniment that cook made for just such reasons. He'd tried to corner her there, but she'd escaped, running to the drawing room, where there was only one escape.

Realizing she'd been trapped like a rat, she'd grabbed up a bust of Julius Caesar and when he'd cornered her again, tearing at her clothes and spewing obscene things from his lips, she'd brought it crashing down on his head. The sickening thud it had made was a sound she'd never forget. The sight of blood welling from his scalp and pouring over his face as he collapsed was also permanently burned into her mind.

"What will we do, m'lady? If he talks and she goes to Bow Street we're done for!"

"If who talks?"

At the sound of Griffin's voice, Olympia glanced up and felt her heart jump into her throat. How much had he heard? She tried to speak, but no sound emerged. Instead, she simply gaped at him before finally managing to close her mouth entirely and shaking her head.

"Collins, leave us," he instructed.

The maid passed the letter back to Olympia and then scurried away quickly. She was clearly terrified and rightly so. Would he send them away? When he learned what she had done would he deliver her to the magistrates himself? It wasn't simply the fear that he would send them away, or even fear of the legal consequences of their crimes. Something in her had awakened at his touch, something more than the passion he spoke of so easily. Since her parents' deaths in that horrible carriage accident, she'd tamped down her emotions, locking them away ruthlessly in self preservation. And yet, when in his presence, she felt giddy almost, giddy and hopeful. She was no longer so all alone in the world, and she very much feared that if he were to spurn her, she would never recover from it. She didn't want him to know the violence she was capable of, for fear that it would alter the way he looked at her. And yet, she did not wish to lie to him.

"Tell me," he implored. "Whatever it is, tell me and I will help you."

"You won't. You can't. You certainly shouldn't. There's no help for what I've done," she admitted grudgingly.

He knelt in front of her, covering her cold and trembling hands with his. "Let me be the judge of that."

When he pried the letter from her fingers, she didn't resist. But she did watch his face as he read the brief missive. At the end, he simply frowned.

"There is nothing in this letter to account for your sudden change in disposition... and yet, I know this is the cause. So why don't you explain to me what all of this really means?"

"I tried to murder my uncle," she said abruptly.

CHAPTER NINETEEN

It was not wholly unexpected, her admission. Not the nature of it, at any rate, but she was clearly surprised to have made a confession at all. Her eyes widened and he could see the panic settling in.

"Why?" he asked.

"Because I'm a horrible person," she said. "Why does anyone commit murder? Because they lack morality!"

Griffin would have laughed at that, but she seemed to be completely sincere in her belief. "You are not a horrible person. Not in the least. You are kind and understanding, and I cannot believe that you would attempt bodily injury to someone who had done nothing to provoke you. So tell me, Olympia, what did your uncle do to you that preceded your attempt to end his life?"

Griffin watched her expression closely. He had a very

good idea what might have prompted it. As she blushed and looked away, her eyes downcast and her lower lip trembling slightly, he knew that he was correct.

"I wish you had succeeded," he said softly. "Any man who would abuse a woman, a relative, in his care, doesn't deserve to live."

"You don't know... I wasn't just defending myself!" she protested.

"I do not know. And that is why you should tell me," he said. "Tell me, so that if the time comes that I need to help you with this, I have the information I need to do so."

"I was in the drawing room... I had run there to get away from him, not thinking that there was only one way in or out," she said haltingly. "And when he came close to me, within reach, I picked up a marble bust from the table and I hit him as hard as I could. There was blood... so much blood."

"Then it was an accident," he said. "You were defending yourself, as is your right."

She looked up then, their gazes locking as her expression grew even bleaker by the second. "No. Once was an accident. Once was self-defense. But then I hit him again. And when he fell to the floor, bleeding and unconscious, I struck him twice more. I wanted him to die. I wanted to never again feel cornered or threatened, or to wonder if the ancient, rickety chair I'd wedged beneath the doorknob would hold through one more night. That is why I am a horrible person... that is why I am morally compromised."

"Do you expect me to judge you for this?" he asked incredulously. "Do you think that it would somehow change my opinion of you to know that you harbored rage for a man who forced you to live in fear? It does not. It will not. You could have struck him a dozen times and shot him for good measure, and I would still say he was deserving."

She blinked at him then. "Then you are a rare man my lord. Most men, while they would be scandalized by his actions, by his inappropriate attraction to his own niece, would never dare to question his behavior... but they would be very quick to judge mine."

"I am not most men... and I don't find his behavior scandalous. I find it reprehensible. Criminal, or at least it should be. Now tell me what part your mouse of a maid played in this."

Olympia glared at him. "She is not a mouse!"

"She's as timid as one when I'm around!"

"Collins helped me move him. To cover up my crime, we tried to make it look as if he fell down the stairs, so we carried him to the foot of the staircase and then cleaned up the blood in the drawing room, though I daresay we didn't get all of it... in fact, I know we didn't. Collins slipped on the wet floor and turned her ankle badly. That was why I had to walk to Darkwood alone that first day."

"Why do you think that?"

"It was dark. We were both terrified," she said, throwing her hands up. "How else would my aunt know?"

"She doesn't know. From the tone of her letter, she may suspect... but you must remember one thing, Olympia."

"What is that?"

"You are now the wife of a Viscount... and whether it is fair or not, in a court of law, if it were to even go that far, my title would count for something," he explained.

"But the scandal—."

"I don't care."

"I could hang for this, Griffin. My aunt and uncle are the type of people who would pursue this to the ends of the earth!"

He rose and pulled her up with him, folding his arms around her. "It will not happen. Whatever it takes, Olympia, I will keep you safe... I promised you that the first day I brought you here and I mean to keep that promise. Trust me?"

"I do," she said. "I do trust you... Thank you."

"Whatever for?"

She leaned into his chest, pressing her face against him. "For believing me, for not judging me, for standing with me regardless of my wrongdoing. I've been so alone, Griffin... no one has believed in me, cared for me in this way, since my parents died. I didn't think anyone would ever again." She paused then, lifted her head and looked up at him with a slight smile. He could see the hint of tears in her dark eyes. "It was the very next morning that I saw the advertisement Mr. Swindon had placed in the paper. I'd never believed in fate... until now. It feels like fate brought me here to you."

He kissed her then, unable to do anything else. He didn't believe in fate, but whatever had brought her to him, he was grateful.

"Mr. Swindon should be arriving in a few days. He will offer your aunt and uncle a settlement... a gesture of goodwill on my part, but it will be made clear to them that my goodwill is contingent upon them never bothering you again."

In the dressing room, with her ear pressed to the door, Mrs. Webster listened. Initially, she'd been thrilled at the confession, but Lord Darke's response chiseled away at her glee until only bitterness remained. The girl was, by her own admission, a murderess, if an incompetent one. Yet still he protected her, vowed to eradicate any consequences of her misdeeds out of some misguided sense of chivalry.

She thought of Lady Florence's suggestion, to use Cassandra to rid them of the interloper. As wrong as it seemed to exploit that poor damaged child, it was even more wrong to let that woman take control of Darkwood Hall, to steal control of the one place she'd always called home.

"I won't have it," she whispered. "I will not allow her to take this from me!"

Using the servant's passageways, she slipped from one

dressing chamber to the other and then exited into the hallway through the master chamber. In the hallway, she came face to face with Lady Florence who waited eagerly for news.

"She's told him her secrets and he'd vowed to do whatever is necessary to protect the worthless chit," Mrs. Webster said.

"I see. So we revert to my original plan," Lady Florence said briskly. "If he will not throw her off because of scandal, we will simply have to find a more permanent way of ridding ourselves of her. You will do what is necessary, Mrs. Webster?"

The housekeeper nodded. "I will, my lady, whatever is necessary."

CHAPTER TWENTY

GRIFFIN CLIMBED the stairs to Cassandra's chamber with a heavy heart. It had been two days since Olympia's confession, two days that had been remarkably peaceful. A letter had arrived from Swindon, stating that he was delayed in London. Griffin had the sneaking suspicious that Swindon was still making himself scarce on purpose. After all, filing for an annulment without his solicitor was hardly a likely occurrence. Of course, an annulment was no longer possible, nor was it wanted, but Swindon had to be aware of all that as soon as Griffin's letter describing the gift he wished to give to Olympia had arrived. But, Griffin reflected, it wasn't the first time Swindon had pointedly ignored his wishes and it undoubtedly would not be the last. But Swindon wasn't his primary concern at the moment.

Whatever changes he'd made to Cassandra's medication

had been working. He'd thought that the formula was finally perfected. She'd been calmer than he'd seen her in years—until a few hours ago. She'd been having a difficult evening. The screaming had begun even before dinner and had only grown in intensity. As he neared the top, he heard the shattering of glass.

As he entered her room, he saw Mrs. Webster desperately sweeping the broken glass from his sister's reach. It was the last vial of the new batch he'd made, the one that had been working so well for her.

"I'm so sorry, my lord. She knocked it from my hand," the housekeeper offered, sounding truly contrite for the loss of the soothing draught.

Cassandra was wilder than he'd seen her in some time, pacing and growling like a caged animal. What went on her mind then, he wondered? Was there any consciousness remaining or had his uncle managed to eradicate all of it with his ill fated attempt on her life? "It's fine, Mrs. Webster. I shall simply make more. It will be at least an hour. Will you give her laudanum to calm her until I return?"

"I can try, my lord. But it only works for a short time on her anymore."

Griffin nodded. "I will hurry as much as possible, but the herbs must cook for the proper amount of time or they will be too potent for her."

"Yes, my lord."

Griffin left the room again, heading for the conservatory

and the small hothouse there so that he could gather what he needed. As he closed the door to the East wing behind him, Lady Florence emerged from a shadowed doorway.

With Griffin gone, she climbed the stairs to Cassandra's chamber. "How much time do we have?" she asked the housekeeper.

"Only an hour. I've given her the laudanum already. It should have her docile enough in a few minutes," Mrs. Webster said.

"We'll place her in Lady Darke's dressing room...Are you sure she'll enter the bed chamber when she awakens?"

"Yes," Mrs. Webster said. "If her ladyship is awake, if she makes any noise at all or if there's light, Cassandra is likely to follow it. This is not a foolproof plan, my lady. There are many ways for it to go wrong."

"She's dismissed her maid already," Lady Florence said. "I saw the girl in the corridor with the dress Lady Darke had worn to dinner. She won't return with it until morning."

By the time they'd finished plotting, Cassandra had slumped against Mrs. Webster, her limbs lax and her mouth slightly agape; her eyes were glazed and distant.

"It's time, Mrs. Webster... once we've placed her, you must return here and make yourself appear injured."

"Yes, my lady. It's already planned out," the housekeeper replied.

Together, the two women dragged the barely conscious Cassandra down the hall and into the main corridor. It was no mean feat to get her into the dressing room without making a sound, but somehow they managed. Settling her onto the small cot there that was sometimes occupied by the maid, they parted ways—Lady Florence to waylay Griffin and delay his return and Mrs. Webster to fake Cassandra's escape.

When I discovered that I was with child, I had thought my life had simply ended. My lover was gone, and surely my new suitor would spurn me the moment he learned the truth. But the Honorable Sir Richard Griffin has proven to be far more charitable than I could ever have dreamed.

He confessed to me today that there is a history of madness in his family, an infirmity of the mind that some are born with and that strikes others much later in their life. Not only has he chosen to accept me, but also to accept my unborn child as his own, an heir, he hopes, that will be free of any taint of the illness that has cursed his family.

Olympia read the passage in the journal again. Still not trusting her eyes or her mind to have interpreted again, she read a third time. It was written plainly in Miss Patrice Landon's handwriting. Griffin, her first born son, was a bastard, but one claimed by her husband and welcomed with joy.

One thought came unbidden then, and it was the most welcome thought she'd ever entertained. She could bear his children. Would he be pleased if she told him? Or would the knowledge of his mother's affair anger him?

Curious to know more, Olympia read on. She read of their marriage and then of Richard's botanical studies. The entries grew fewer and further between, sometimes months would be missing. It wasn't until Patrice wrote of her second child, a girl that was damaged, that Olympia abruptly closed the book. The woman's pain had been profound and her belief that the child's mental defect was in some way her punishment was too horrible to contemplate.

A noise in the dressing room gave her a start, lost in thought as she was. Assuming it was Collins, she settled back into her chair and considered her options. She could tell Griffin but that would require a confession on her part— that she had in fact been lurking and spying, just as Mrs. Webster had once accused her. Though in light of what she had to disclose and what it could mean for both of them, she had to believe that he wouldn't be overly angry or if he was, it would surely give way to relief when he realized that he was free from the fear of losing his own sanity.

Another noise from the dressing room brought her up on alert. The smashing of glass was not something she'd expected to hear. "Collins?" she called out. There was no answer.

Olympia got to her feet. She could hear the blood rushing

in her ears and taste the bitter tang of fear on her tongue. Her hand trembled as she reached out and placed it against the dressing room door. Even as she reached for the knob, it turned. Another sound came from beyond that door, the low keening wail that she'd come to recognize. Cassandra had been freed from her tower.

When the door started to open, Olympia threw all of her weight against it. She struggled to keep it closed, but the young woman on the other side of it was impossibly strong, enraged beyond the point of reason or return. Olympia screamed out for help, but she had to wonder if it was a futile effort. Everyone at Darkwood Hall had become inured to the sounds of screams in the night. Would hers even be heard or would they simply be dismissed as a familiar night sound in this strange house?

The door reverberated painfully against her shoulder as Cassandra continued to throw herself against it. How long would it hold? Was there enough intellect left in the girl for her to figure out that there was another way into the room? Olympia had no sooner thought it than the continuous thumping stopped.

But it wasn't movement at the main door to her chamber that prompted her fear to soar to new heights. It was the acrid scent of smoke.

Fire.

"Oh, God!" Olympia muttered as she reached out and tested the door handle. It was already warm to the touch.

Panic set in. She had no idea what to do... which way was safe?

G RIFFIN CRUSHED chamomile leaves to add to the tonic he'd developed for Cassandra. It had been a long process of trial and error, of experimentation, before he'd discovered the right combination of herbs that would calm her without simply sending her to sleep.

As the mixture steeped, he placed the palms of his hands flat on the work table, let his chin drop to his chest and tried to will away his exhaustion. Mrs. Webster's words came back to him. Some things, once broken, could not be repaired. Holding on to the hope that Cassandra would regain any of her mental functioning was perhaps the most hopelessly mad thing he'd ever done.

She'd always been fragile, her mind never quite developing at the same rate of other children's. Then, as the years had progressed and he'd learned the true extent of his uncle's abuses towards her, not just the pinches, shoves and slaps he'd visited on all of them, but his other, more perverse desires, Griffin had wanted to murder him. It had been that knowledge, that awful discovery that had prompted Griffin's own father into that last deep melancholy that had preceded his suicide.

His mother had begged him not to act, pointing out that

they were now financially dependent on his father's brother, Viscount Darke. Griffin hadn't cared, he'd boasted that he could work, he would obtain employment. She'd calmly pointed out that he'd be in prison and she would have to work, which meant Cassandra would have to be placed in an asylum.

He'd seen the validity of her point, though it had goaded him horribly. But as the months had worn on and his uncle had grown more and more irrational, his moods more violent, he'd wondered if they weren't courting disaster by remaining at Darkwood, even in the relative safety of the dower house.

Pushing away those thoughts, recognizing them as an exercise in futility, he rose to his full height, only to see Florence standing in the doorway. She'd never come to the conservatory before, certainly never to his small workroom in the back.

"What are you doing here?"

"I've come to visit," she said with a coy smile. "Don't be so mean, Griffin. You used to enjoy my company... once upon a time."

He had no patience for her. Exhausted beyond all reason, her cat and mouse games were too much. "Once upon a time," he replied, "I was unaware that you were a vicious, grasping harlot."

She didn't take offense. He'd learned long ago that any display of emotion from Florence was entirely manufactured.

The woman was completely without feeling, unless one counted greed and vanity. Those she had in abundance.

"Is that any way to greet me when I've come to offer you my silence?"

"You are incapable of silence. You will forever yammer on until even the dead wish to tune you out."

"Well, your charming new wife's uncle isn't dead, is he? In spite of her best efforts."

Griffin had been ignoring her, tidying up his work space and preparing to bottle the elixir. At he words, he stopped immediately and faced her. "Spying are you?"

"Not me personally, no. But Mrs. Webster is rather good at it. She filled me in on all the gory details... Such a blood-thirsty little thing, your bride. I do believe Darkwood Hall might be perfect for her after all!"

"What are you after, Florence? I've given you a great allowance... I'll hire a stable of handsome footmen for you. What more could you ask for?" he demanded.

She smiled. "London. You're going to secure a house for me, a wardrobe fit for a queen... and I'm going husband hunting. Rich, old, feeble."

"And here I thought strapping young lads from the country were more your cup of tea," Griffin uttered sarcastically.

"Only for lovers. For husbands I have a different set of criteria altogether. I learned a lot of lessons from my first disastrous marriage. I was sadly disappointed by your uncle. I had thought him too old and too infirm for the marriage bed. How bitterly disappointed I was when he proved me wrong night after night. He was nearly insatiable. You've no need to hate me or want revenge against me for jilting you. Suffering his attentions nightly was torment enough."

"Fine, Florence," he relented. He was too tired to argue with her about it. "You may have a house in London, you may have a fleet of willing men. Any expense would be worth it not to have to bear your presence here."

Her eyebrows rose in a clear expression of surprise. "Oh, dear. I hadn't thought you'd relent so easily," she said. "I believe your new wife has made you soft... in a manner of speaking."

Bored with her double entendres and her smug tone, Griffin simply poured the elixir he'd created into a new vial. "I need to get this to Mrs. Webster. Good night, Florence."

She approached him then, placing her hand on his chest. Every movement of her lithe body was intended to seduce. Swaying hips, sultry languorous steps, and her wrapper conveniently falling from one shoulder to reveal the upper swell of her breast. "We enjoyed each other once, didn't we?"

"Once," he agreed, completely unmoved by her display. "But that was before I understood precisely what you are... and precisely what you lack."

Her lips formed a pretty pout. "You told me once that I was the most beautiful woman in the world. What could I possibly be lacking?"

"A heart and a conscience," he said evenly. "Now, let me pass, Florence. I must attend my sister!"

Griffin was prepared to move her bodily from his path, but there was a commotion in the hall beyond. Servants began running and shouting. He heard one word that made his blood run cold. Fire.

It all made perfect sense to him in that moment. She was there to keep him occupied, so that whatever elaborate plot she and the housekeeper had cooked up could be carried out in his absence. "What have you done?" he asked in horror, but he did not wait for her answer. He shoved past her and raced toward the stairs.

CHAPTER TWENTY-ONE

OLYMPIA HAD MANAGED to open the door to the dressing room by using her shawl to protect her hand. As she peered through the flames, she could see no one in the room. If Cassandra had truly been in there, and she couldn't imagine who else would have been, who else would have been able to replicate that strange and haunting cry, she was no longer. On the far side of the small room, she could see that the window was broken. Had that been the sound of breaking glass she'd heard?

Dread washed through her. No one could survive such a fall. Servants began to race in the hall behind her. Someone outside or possibly in the stables must have seen the flames and raised the alarm she realized.

A rather brawny footman pulled her back out of the way, as he and several others rushed to put out the flames. Buckets of sand and water were dumped on the worst of it while another man ripped burning clothes and curtains and tossed them from the window.

"It won't catch anything else on fire, m'lady! There's a small spring runs by that side of the house. Everything stays damp there."

The reassurance had been offered by Marjorie, the young maid who had attended her on her first day at Darkwood Hall. It had been little more than a week in all and yet it seemed a lifetime ago.

Griffin came tearing into the room. When he saw her, he stopped short. His eyes roamed over her as if taking in every detail and then, almost before she could process the look of intense relief on his face, he jumped into the fray, battling back the stubborn flames.

Collins came rushing in and Mrs. Webster was at her heels. Mrs. Webster saw the flames and began scanning the room. Watching her, Olympia realized she was looking for one person specifically.

Cassandra hadn't simply escaped her chamber. She'd been deliberately set free to injure her, or worse. Her suspicions were confirmed when Mrs. Webster fell to her knees and began to weep.

"What's the matter with her?" Collins asked.

"Guilt," Olympia replied succinctly.

The fire was rather anticlimactic once everyone had arrived. The small dressing room was comprised of stone walls, and because her wardrobe was so limited, there was little enough in the room to feed the flames. Any remaining fabric or upholstery had been tossed out the broken window, along with the carpet. The room was emptied of everything but a blackened marble wash-stand. The walls were stained with black smoke and streaked from the rivulets of water that had run down them.

Griffin emerged. His shirt sleeves were singed and black-ened, his hair was mussed, but it was the expression he wore that terrified her. He was focused solely on Mrs. Webster who still wept on the floor. Not a soul had offered her comfort.

"Griffin—."

"She did this," he interrupted her. "She and Florence engineered all of this!"

"I do not doubt it," she said softly. "But Griffin, they didn't set the fire."

"Then who did?" he asked.

Olympia looked at him, stared up into the harsh planes of his face. She had only an inkling of all the losses that he'd suffered in his life, but even that was overwhelming. The very idea of uttering the words left her shaken, and yet she had to tell him. Taking a deep steadying breath, she spoke quickly. "It was Cassandra... I don't think they meant for this to happen. Not the fire. But I think they set her free with the intent that she would do me harm."

His face hardened, the muscles in his jaw clenching tightly. "Where is she now?"

"When I got the door open finally, she wasn't in the room," Olympia said. Tears flowed freely and she was struggling to speak clearly through the sobs that threatened. "But the window was already broken."

He said nothing for what seemed like ages. The whole room, which had previously been abuzz, went utterly still. Then he simply brushed past her, past the weeping and sobbing form of Mrs. Webster and made for the stairs.

Olympia gathered as much of her composure as possible, and urged several of the footmen, "Go with him. He may need your help."

They looked at Mrs. Webster, as if waiting for her to countermand the order, but she was beyond such thoughts. Then, after a heartbeat's pause, they followed him down the stairs and out into the night.

"Let's get you out of this smoky room, m'lady. It can't be good for you," Collins urged.

"The letters and the journal, Collins... Get them from the desk," she said. It was imperative, given the sensitive information they contained, that they not fall into either Florence's hands or Mrs. Webster's when she was recovered enough to even care for such matters.

The maid nodded her agreement, and once she'd secured the items, they made their way downstairs to the drawing room. Dressed only in her wrapper and night rail, Olympia realized that was literally all she owned. Her meager wardrobe was gone entirely. But others had lost so much more. Thinking of Griffin, of what he must be going through, Olympia had to sit down. She couldn't bear to think of what he must be suffering, to know that he would undoubtedly blame himself for everything when clearly there were only two people at fault in the entirely horrific chain of events. Mrs. Webster and Lady Florence were the ones to blame.

"Marjorie," Olympia instructed, "Have another room prepared for Lord Darke and myself, as our suite will be unin-habitable."

"Yes, m'lady," the maid said. She paused at the door, "Only one chamber, m'lady?"

"One will suffice," she confirmed.

The maid blushed and nodded her agreement before scurrying off to do as she'd been bidden. With nothing else to be done, Olympia simply waited for the inevitable—for Griffin to return with his sister's body.

SHE'D FALLEN into the spring. If there'd been any blood, it had already washed away. But it was clear to him that her neck had simply snapped. It was a consolation, albeit a small one, that she had not suffered.

Griffin waded into the shallow water and lifted her gently. The footmen were there to assist him, sent by

Olympia no doubt, as Mrs. Webster had clearly been in no condition to command the servants. Guilt was a terrible thing. He'd carried it for years and it would undoubtedly plague him for the rest of his days. Now she understood what that felt like.

As he carried her back to the house, he realized that it was quite possibly the last thing he would ever do for his sister. He had no family left. They were all gone.

There were no tears to shed. Perhaps he should have wept, but the overwhelming sense of relief he felt shamed him. He missed the Cassandra of his childhood, he missed the girl she'd been, but he did not and could not miss the wild and volatile creature she'd become. He grieved for her, but that did not change the fact that a heavy burden had been lifted from him. He didn't deserve the release of tears, he thought.

The door was opened for him and he carried her into the house and up the stairs into one of the unoccupied bed chambers. Several of the maids were there, clearly confused about who she was, as they'd all been hired long after she'd been banished to the far reaches of the East wing.

He laid her on the bed, heedless of the wet gown she wore. Still he drew the covers over her. "Ready her for burial. It will be done in the morning," he said stiffly, and then simply walked out. He could hear the maids whispering behind him, asking who she was and where she'd come from. Answering their questions was beyond him, explaining the tragedy of who she was and what had ruined her so completely was simply beyond him.

Olympia was standing at the top of the stairs. "Are you—no," she said. "I won't even ask how you are. The answer is obvious... I am so terribly sorry, Griffin. If I'd known that she would jump—."

"Do not," he said, cutting her off. "Nothing that has occurred here tonight is your fault."

"I was too afraid to open the door, but if I had, she might have survived."

"Or you would have died," he said. "Since her injury, she had no perception of pain or exhaustion. It was all just rage with her."

She walked toward him slowly and took his hand in hers. "Come. I've had them prepare a chamber for us for tonight."

He allowed her to lead him into their temporary chamber. "It's my fault," he said. "It's my fault that she was injured at all. It's my fault that Mrs. Webster and Lady Florence were here to exploit her the way that they did."

"How is it your fault?" she demanded. "How, when you've done everything in your power to care for her and to help her, to make her better, is it possibly your fault?"

"Because when I found out what my uncle was doing to her... that he was cut from the very same cloth that your own uncle is, I didn't insist that we leave this house. I allowed my mother to convince me that we should remain here. And then when my uncle had his final breakdown, he murdered both of his sons in the dining room and attempted to put a pistol ball in her brain as well."

OLYMPIA TRIED to absorb the impact of what he'd just said, but it was too much. "Oh, Griffin... that wasn't your fault."

He sat down on the bed, defeated, his shoulders slumped forward and his head resting in his hands. It looked as if the events of the night had simply been too much for him to bear, as strong as he was. Uncertain what else to do and desperate to do anything that would help him, she moved toward him and closed her arms around him. He accepted the embrace, locking his arms around her thighs and holding her to him.

"He thought he'd killed her, you see," he explained. "But apparently the gun misfired in some way, or it simply didn't have enough powder in it. The ball didn't penetrate her skull, but it did enough damage regardless... Enough damage that there were times when I believed she would have been so much better off had he succeeded."

There was nothing to say in response to that, so she continued to hold him, stroking his hair and letting him speak. Finally, she managed, "You did everything you could for her, Griffin. There was no way to predict your uncle's behavior, there was no way to predict what Lady Florence and Mrs. Webster would do tonight. What we have to do now is determine how we will deal with them."

He looked up at her. "I can't think about them. If I think about them tonight, I'll do murder. Her life had been brutal enough without them using her so basely and letting her meet such a miserable end."

"Then we won't think about them tonight. We'll deal with them in the morning... for tonight, you will rest. You were exhausted to begin with and I cannot imagine what this has been like for you."

Griffin settled his head against her, resting it just beneath her breasts. Olympia held him there, offering what comfort she could.

"I have no other family," he said. "They are all gone now... cousins, sibling, parents. I am the last. It was what I had wanted—to ensure this madness ended with me, but I hadn't realized that it would feel so very lonely."

She had to tell him, Olympia realized, to disclose what she'd discovered in the letters and journal. It had initially seemed like such a terrible time, but given what he'd just said, she wondered if perhaps the information wouldn't offer him some peace.

"Griffin, Mrs. Webster had accused me of spying and lurking," she began. "And she was correct. I have been lurking and spying... and I took something that wasn't mine."

He leaned back and planted his hands on the bed so that he could meet her gaze. "I am beyond tired, Olympia. If there is some point to this, it needs to be made very clearly because I am unable to put the facts together myself."

"I found your mother's journal and some letters… they were hidden in a trunk in the East wing. And your father… rather, the man you thought was your father, well, he wasn't."

He blinked at her. "It isn't any clearer, Olympia."

"Your mother was involved with a man, a soldier based on the letters I read. She was intimate with him… and you were the result."

"She lied to her husband—."

"No. He knew," Olympia said. "He knew right from the start and he accepted you gladly. His reasoning was that he would have an heir, he would have a son who would be spared the melancholy and the madness that had plagued the rest of your family… And he loved you, Griffin, as if you were his. Do not ever think otherwise."

He said nothing for the longest time. Olympia searched his face for any indication that he'd heard her, much less understood the gravity of what she'd just said to him.

"Griffin? Did you hear me?"

He closed his arms around her, holding her so tightly that she could scarcely breathe. There was a desperation in him as he clung to her.

"I heard you," he whispered. "You're certain?"

"Yes," Olympia replied. "Quite sure. I have the letters and the journal if you want to read them, though the content is perhaps more risqué than one would wish to associate with one's mother."

He shuddered then, but chuckled softly as she'd

intended. "I'll defer to your judgement then." Griffin drew a deep breath, "I'm not going to go mad. The thing I've feared my entire adult life is not going to happen."

She smiled. "No. You will not go mad. Well, I might drive you to it... but not like your father, not like your uncle, and not like poor Cassandra. That is one burden you can shake off."

"Let us go to bed," he said. "I cannot think anymore tonight, I simply cannot take anything else in. Tomorrow will be soon enough to sort everything out."

Olympia could not have agreed more. She climbed into the bed with him. A sigh escaped her as he pulled her close, holding her against him. It wasn't about passion or desire. It was about comfort, about being there for one another. Turning into his embrace, she laid her head against his shoulder and closed her arms around him. They slept that way, holding one another through the night.

CHAPTER TWENTY-TWO

FLORENCE WAS WASTING no time in making the necessary preparations for her getaway. Staying at Darkwood Hall was no longer an option. Griffin would be furious, furious enough that he might actually be beyond caring about the scandals she and Mrs. Webster could bring to light. Retreat, for the moment, was her only option.

She did actually still have a friend or two in Liverpool. Her statement to the contrary had only been to avoid having him send her away before she'd discovered what she needed to about his new bride.

Mrs. Webster, she thought, as she tossed another chemise and petticoat into her bag, was another matter altogether. The woman, in spite of her cold demeanor, had actually cared deeply for Cassandra. With the horrible events that had unfolded after their plan went awry, it was anyone's guess what the housekeeper would do. She didn't mean to be there to find out. It was one of the reasons she'd elected to pack her own bag rather than asking for the assistance of one of the maids. She didn't want any of the servants to be privy to her escape until it was underway. Only her personal maid was aware of her plan and she meant to keep it that way.

The door opened, but she didn't turn around, assuming it was her maid returning with the items she'd requested. "Leave my green traveling gown, Parks, and pack the rest," she said.

"That won't be necessary, Lady Florence. You won't be going anywhere."

Florence had been stuffing clothing items into her bag, but at the sound of that voice, she stopped, going completely still. Taking a calming breath, she turned to face her co-conspirator. "Mrs. Webster," she acknowledged. The tidy and incredibly severe woman she was acquainted with had vanished. In her place as a ravaged creature, her face streaked with tears, hair wild, clothing disheveled. But it was the absence of the cold and reserved expression she normally wore that was truly telling. In its place was a murderous rage, a wildness that reminded her of a feral animal.

"I knew better," the woman said. "I knew better than to go along with your ridiculous scheme...Because of us, that poor girl is gone. Even mad, I can't help but fear that suicide is a mortal sin."

"It wasn't suicide," Florence said sharply. "The poor, daft

thing hadn't a clue what she was doing. Suicide implies intent!"

"Like our intent? To use her and exploit her, to take what the last Lord Darke did to her and use it for our own gain?"

"If Griffin would have married me we wouldn't have had to do any of it! It's *his* fault... All of it is his fault," Florence protested. "If we're lucky, this will be the last straw for him. It'll drive him mad, he'll take his own life and hers... and then I'll marry that distant cousin of his and together we will rule this house as we were meant to! It was your birthright! When Roger's father forced himself upon your mother, when she bore you in this house where she served, you earned it. Do not falter now."

Mrs. Webster shook her head, "I've been listening to you since you first came here—letting your feed my bitterness, stoking it like a flame until it consumed me entirely. No more."

The housekeeper's expression hardened. There was a resolve in her that was utterly terrifying, but Florence reminded herself that the woman was a servant, and servants would always do as they were told. It was simply the way of their world.

Attempting to brazen it out, Florence laughed bitterly. "What do you plan to do? Confess? He knows. He's guessed already that it was the two of us who led Cassandra to Lady Darke's dressing room!"

"I don't mean to confess, Lady Florence. I mean to atone.

We're going to pay for what we did to her," Mrs. Webster said, walking towards her.

As she neared, Florence saw that she held a brace of pistols, one in each hand. "What are you doing? Stop this at once."

Mrs. Webster raised the first gun, leveling it at her. Florence had no time to beg, no time to plead for her life or for forgiveness. The pistol ball ripped through her bodice and she fell to the floor with a shrill scream.

As she lay there, bleeding on the carpet, Mrs. Webster lifted the second pistol and placed it to her head. Florence closed her eyes as she heard the report of the weapon.

THE SOUND of gunfire pulled her from sleep. Olympia sat up with a start, but Griffin slept on. Reluctantly, she jostled his shoulder. It didn't work. She repeated it again, more forcefully. Finally, he opened his eyes.

"What is it?" he asked groggily.

No sooner had he asked the question than another shot rang out. "Griffin, I think something awful has happened."

He rose immediately, reaching for his shirt and the still damp breeches he'd discarded. After he'd dressed hurriedly, he left the room. Servants were appearing in the hall, coming down from the floor above where most of them slept.

"Where did that sound come from?" he asked.

One of the maids pointed to Lady Florence's door. "Mine and Marjorie's room is just above hers, m'lord."

"How can you be sure?"

The maid blushed furiously. "Well, we can hear her when she's.... entertaining, m'lord."

Griffin sighed. "Of course." Without saying anything further, he took two long strides and then banged on the door.

"Florence?"

She called out weakly, though the words were unintelligible. Griffin opened the door and cursed immediately. Charging into the room, he didn't bother to check Mrs. Webster. It was glaringly apparent based on the nature of her wound that the woman could not possibly have survived.

He moved toward Florence. She lay in a pool of blood that was spreading rapidly around her. He moved to lift her but she screamed out in pain.

"Don't," she said. "Don't. It's too late."

"Florence, we can send for the doctor!"

"We both know I've lost too much blood already," she said. "Mrs. Webster—."

"Don't try to talk."

"I have to tell you," she insisted. "She was Roger's half sister... his father forced himself upon her mother when she worked here."

It all made more sense then, Mrs. Webster's obsession with control of Darkwood Hall and her resentment of him and everyone else in the house who had a legitimate claim to it. But there was no time for more questions. Florence's eyes fluttered closed and her breathing stilled.

Griffin stared down at the body and simply felt numb. So much had happened that he couldn't actually generate an appropriate emotional response. That part of him had simply shut down altogether.

He heard Olympia's gasp from the doorway. "She's gone," he said softly. "Both of them are."

"Shall I send for the magistrate, m'lord?" one of the footmen asked.

Simms, the normally dour but unflappable butler stepped forward. "There is no need to send for a magistrate, Thomas. 'Twas a terrible tragedy that the three of them succumbed to a fever... and on the same night as the fire. A terrible tragedy."

"But—." Thomas was cut off abruptly before he could finish his question by a chorus of 'ayes'.

"An awful tragedy, m'lord," Marjorie said. "The fever was just too much for all of them."

Another chorus of ayes. But Griffin shook his head. "I cannot ask you all to lie."

"Begging your pardon, m'lord," Marjorie replied, "But you didn't ask us to do anything of the sort. We've been following Mrs. Webster's orders, God rest her, for as long as we've been here, even when those orders felt wrong somehow. It's time that we started serving the true master and mistress of this house."

Griffin had nothing to say to that. Nothing at all. "We'll

hold services for all of them tomorrow. Can you prepare them?"

Marjorie gulped, but then nodded. "We can, m'lord. We will. You should rest now. It's been a trying day."

Griffin rose and walked toward Olympia who was standing at the door, her arms wrapped about herself as if to ward off a chill. "You shouldn't be seeing this," he said. "You've suffered enough shocks of your own tonight. Let's go to bed. We can take care of all of this tomorrow."

She nodded her agreement and he ushered her back to the chamber they'd taken for the night. With everything that had happened, with all that had changed and shifted so completely in his world since she'd arrived, he could still say without question, that he was infinitely glad that she was there with him. She offered him a kind of peace he'd never known, and he never wanted to let that go.

EPILOGUE

GRIFFIN ENTERED the library and found Olympia there, her nose buried in a book as pale wintry light streamed in through the windows. It had been nearly two weeks since the horrible events had unfolded that had robbed Cassandra of her life and that had led to Mrs. Webster taking Florence's life and her own. He'd made peace with those things, of a sort.

Guilt still plagued him, but more for Cassandra's life than for her death. He'd come to see her death as a way of giving her peace from the demons that had tormented her so.

Olympia looked up at him and smiled. "Where have you been all morning?"

"I went into the village," he said. "I had Swindon order something for me in London and it was delivered to John Short this morning. He sent a message by his son to come fetch it."

She frowned at that. "Why wouldn't he just deliver it himself?"

Griffin smiled as he settled onto the window seat beside her. "It was not the sort of thing one would entrust a twelve year old boy to deliver," he said. Reaching into his pocket, he produced a small wooden box, small enough that it would fit into the palm of his hand. "I realized that you did not have a proper wedding ring, only that cheap band that Swindon had given you... I felt it was time, since you are my wife in every sense of the word, that you had something to mark it."

Olympia's hands trembled as he placed the box in her palm. But it wasn't nerves. It was excitement, she was all but bouncing in her seat. "I can't recall the last time I was given a present," she said, her eyes alight with happiness.

His expression soured at that. "Soon you will not be able to remember a time when you were not receiving them."

She opened the box and gasped. The ring was a large and heavy emerald, haloed with alternating diamonds and pearls. "Oh, Griffin! It's lovely."

"*You* are lovely," he said. "And *you* are *loved*."

She'd been removing the ring from the box, eager to slip it on her finger. But at his words she paused, growing unnaturally still. "What did you say?"

"I said, wife, that you are loved... Is it any wonder that I've fallen madly in love with you? That somehow, in this house of horrors, you have brought light and laughter to me when I thought both lost forever?"

She launched herself at him, her arms closing about his neck as she pressed a kiss to his lips. "I love you so much," she said. "I didn't dare to hope that you'd love me in return... Fondness, affection... and you've made your desire for me quite evident, but I didn't think to expect love."

"Whether you expected it or not, it is yours forever," he vowed, holding her close. "And I've been thinking about our initial agreement... The impediment to us having children, the fear that I might somehow pass on the madness that afflicts this family, is no more. And I very much want to have children with you, Olympia. I want that more than anything."

"Of course! I want that to... The very idea of it gives me joy," she said. "I don't want this house to be filled with darkness and ugly memories. I want to fill it with new and happy ones... What better way to do that than with the laughter of children?"

"Then come upstairs with me," he urged, smiling roguishly as he stood and tugged at her hand.

She blushed. "*Griffin!* It's the middle of the day! The servants will be scandalized!"

"They'll grow used to it," he replied. "Come upstairs with me and let us see what we can do about filling this house with children."

He saw her waver. Even as the blush on her cheeks burned brighter, she slipped the ring he'd given her on her finger and then placed her hand in his. He was still smiling as he led her from the room, up the stairs, and past the smug and knowing glances of the butler, Simms, and their new house-keeper, Miss Marjorie Jones.

THE END

IF YOU ENJOYED *A Love So Dark*, the remaining novels in the Dark Regency Series are available at all major retailers. They may be read in sequence or as standalone novels.

Thank you for reading.

MAILING LIST

If you'd like to be notified when I have a new release or a sale on backlist titles, please sign up for my mailing list at the link below:

http://eepurl.com/b9B7lL

The Vanishing of Lord Vale

The Missing Marquess of Althorn

The Resurrection of Lady Ramsleigh

The Mystery of Miss Mason

The Awakening of Lord Ambrose

ABOUT THE AUTHOR

Chasity Bowlin grew up in Tennessee watching soap operas and Scooby Doo in equal measure, both of which fueled her love of gothic romance! She lives in Central Kentucky with her husband who consistently has at least seven home improvement projects going at any one time and their menagerie of animals. She also loves to hear from her readers and can be contacted at either chasitybowlin@gmail.com or at www.facebook.com/chasitybowlin.

Made in the USA
Middletown, DE
26 December 2021

57050523R00144